A History of Hazardous Objects

The New Oeste Series

León Salvatierra and Daniel A. Olivas, *Series Editors*

The New Oeste series celebrates the outpouring of creative expression by Latinx writers in the American West of the twenty-first century. In border-breaking literary arts informed by perspectives as distinctive as the American West, the authors in the series explore the artistic, cultural, and intellectual connections between the region's complicated past and its diverse future. With a commitment to the power of prose and poetry to unite, educate, and enrich, the series editors seek to support projects from unique voices that invite connection and inclusion within the American West. Currently, the editors seek fiction, poetry, and creative nonfiction that expand conceptions of the West and its people.

Preparatory Notes for Future Masterpieces: A Novel
Maceo Montoya

The World Doesn't Work That Way, but It Could
Yxta Maya Murray

How to Date a Flying Mexican: New and Collected Stories
Daniel A. Olivas

To the North/Al norte: Poems
León Salvatierra

*My Chicano Heart: New and Collected
Stories of Love and Other Transgressions*
Daniel A. Olivas

A History of Hazardous Objects: A Novel
Yxta Maya Murray

A History of
Hazardous Objects

A NOVEL

YXTA MAYA MURRAY

UNIVERSITY OF NEVADA PRESS | *Reno & Las Vegas*

University of Nevada Press | Reno, Nevada 89557 USA
www.unpress.nevada.edu
Copyright © 2024 by Yxta Maya Murray

Manufactured in the United States of America
FIRST PRINTING
Cover design by Trudi Gershinov/TG Design
Cover art © by Anne Austin Pearce

Library of Congress Cataloging-in-Publication Data
    Names: Murray, Yxta Maya, author.
    Title: A history of hazardous objects : a novel / Yxta Maya Murray.
Description: Reno, Nevada : University of Nevada Press, [2024] |
Summary: "A History of Hazardous Objects, set during the panic and
pain of September 2020, is about family, love, and science. A story
about a Latina radar astronomer who tries to keep her family alive
during Covid, the trauma of racial violence, and the 2020 wildfires,
the novel details how human beings rise above catastrophe."
—Provided by publisher.
    Identifiers: LCCN 2024003486 | ISBN 9781647791636 (paperback) |
ISBN 9781647791643 (ebook)
    Subjects: LCSH: Women astronomers—California—Fiction. |
Hispanic American Women—California—Fiction. | COVID-19
Pandemic, 2020—Fiction. | Racism—Fiction. | Wildfires—
California—Fiction. | LCGFT: Novels.
    Classification: LCC PS3563.U832 H57 2024 | DDC 813/.54—
dc23/eng/20240221
    LC record available at https://lccn.loc.gov/2024003486
ISBN 978-1-64779-163-6 (paper)
ISBN 978-1-64779-164-3 (ebook)
LCCN 2024003486

The paper used in this book meets the requirements of American
National Standard for Information Sciences—Permanence of Paper
for Printed Library Materials, ANSI/NISO Z39.48–1992 (R2002).

This is a work of fiction. The author has been inspired by the careers
and lives of several scientists and one layperson who have figured
importantly in the history of minor planets. Leonid Kulik, Luis
Alvarez, Gerald Wasserburg, and Roy A. Tucker made crucial
findings about asteroids and meteorites in the twentieth and early
twenty-first centuries. Ann Hodges was hit by a meteorite at her
Alabama home in 1954. These people's life stories are engaged in the
book, and the personages are rendered as characters through the
invention of dialogue, scenes, and dynamics with the license called
for by the novelist's art. These are created, imagined figures who may
feel like living souls to their creator but are instead, in the words of
Jorge Luis Borges, unreal "verbal textures."

To Héctor Tobar

Contents

A History of Hazardous Objects

1
Brother Death

"This is a difficult thing for me to tell you, but I need you always to be a little afraid," my mother said. It was 1983. I was seven years old and absorbedly reading a library copy of *Topics in Contemporary Mathematics*. Mom and I sat out on the flowerpot-covered back porch of our apartment building. She rested from a long day working at a hospital cafeteria by drinking Diet Coke and inspecting her lavender and poppy plants, her eyes made mesmerizing by an intricate application of kohl. Releasing her crow-black hair from its chignon, she took the book from me, and went on. "When a girl's young and very smart, like you are, or beautiful, like I was, she thinks that everything will be more perfect as the years go on. But life will only become more dangerous. And that's why you must protect yourself, Laura. Because there's no safe place in the whole world.

"There is no safe place. Not in the palaces where the queens wear jewels, not in the caves where the peasant women starve, and not in the hotels where virgin girls pour wine for drunkards. In every corner there's wickedness waiting to get you, and that's because the world was cursed long before you were born.

"My own mother once told me a story about the fate of this

poor damned planet. This was back when I was your age, before she pawned me off on that bastard and no-good George Vincent Brooks, on whose name I now spit. My beloved mother explained to me that people like Mr. George Vincent Brooks— on whose name I also fart and piss because of the day he brought me a red rose and destroyed my life—were planted among us like evil seeds after a heavenly misery ruined Paradise a billion years ago. Before that disaster came, she said, the First People lived in peace, fishing and laughing all day long like ignoramuses. But this happiness existed only because our ancestors were too stupid to fear the future.

"Far above the sweet earth lived three gods: Sister Night and her twin brothers, Death and Fire. For five thousand years Night, Death, and Fire ruled all the planets in harmony until the day when the brothers decided that they were big guys and didn't want to share power with a woman anymore. Poor Sister Night could tell by the way those pendejos whispered behind their hands that they plotted against her, and so she set a trap. She pretended to get tangled in the Big Dipper, crying out, 'Help, help!' while struggling in the stars. The two man gods crept up to Night, smiling their terrible smiles. Brother Fire hit her across the mouth so that Sister Night spat out drops of blood that turned into meteors. Brother Death punched her in the stomach so that her tears flew across the universe, making new galaxies.

"Sister Night leapt out from the Big Dipper! She twisted her huge arms around her brothers' throats and kicked them in the balls. Brother Fire was thrown back so hard by her karate chops that he tumbled off the top of the Morning Star and fell through space toward Earth. Brother Death screamed for mercy, but Sister Night strangled him and threw him after Brother Fire.

"Brother Fire shouted, '¡Chinga tu madre!' while dropping through the darkness until he hit headfirst onto Chicxulub, where the First People were happily singing and feasting like dummies.

The ocean boiled, and the ground exploded, carving a giant hole into the coast. Almost all the tarpons vanished from the water and the rains turned to acid. The women of the tribe, made bananas by hunger, sold everything they had. Soon, they even traded their baby daughters for food or a little money, sending these children to the ugly cities where bad husbands slithered, until the girls ran away to the United States, which stinks even worse of the hex of Brother Fire.

"And so it is still. Laurita, know that in every house, and every country, no matter how high the walls, there's danger, because that devil came down from the skies and crashed into the earth."

"But wait," I'd asked, staring up at the gold stain the streetlamps spread into the night air. "What happened to Brother Death?"

My mother took a sip of her cola. "Oh, he's still falling through space. Pretty soon, he'll land here, too."

On the evening of June 19, 2004, Roy A. Tucker, David J. Tholen, and Fabrizio Bernardi stood before the immense Bok telescope at Kitt Peak National Observatory, a sculptural white monolith located on a tall blue mountain in Arizona's Sonoran Desert. At Kitt Peak's busy, beeping telescope workstation, the scientists tinkered with an intricacy of dials and switches. Overhead lights dimmed; the observatory's high green dome slid open. A glistening veil of stars appeared.

Tucker, a 53-year-old amateur astronomer and Vietnam War veteran, consulted with Tholen and Bernardi, both researchers at the University of Hawai`i. The men fixed the telescope on a guide star close to the location where Tholen and Bernardi had seen, a few months earlier, a new glimmering smear in the deeper reaches of space. Tucker imagined that on this night he might confirm an unknown object's existence, maybe seeing it in the form of an opaline cloud or a comet's faint tail. It would be an understatement to say that he'd witnessed extraordinary sights before. Three decades previously, Tucker had directed the sky-fall trajectories of cluster bombs as an Air Force sergeant stationed in Thailand, and since then, kept his attention on the heavens. He enjoyed an almost silent career as an electro-optical engineer at the University of Arizona, and it was only in his off hours that he committed himself to his life's passion: At this point in his life, he'd detected more than five hundred minor planets, most of which he spotted at an observatory he hand-built in his Tucson backyard.

Tucker peered through the Bok's eyepiece. His vision adjusted to the black chasm of the galaxy and its flashes and wrinkles of brightness. Suddenly, a new, twinkling body matching Tholen and Bernardi's descriptions emerged to the left of the guide star. This object clipped forward at a rapid trot.

It was an asteroid. The rock careened across space. Made of iron, hypersthene, and feldspar, it spanned an area as large as three and a half football fields.

It appeared to head in the direction of Earth.

Tucker's asteroid disappeared soon after he saw it. He, Tholen, and Bernardi continued sifting the sky, but the rock, now named 2004 MN4, remained incognito for months. Finally, on December 18, an off-the-grid iconoclast and stargazer named Gordon J. Garradd located it from the Siding Spring Observatory in New South Wales, Australia.

Over the next few days, fresh optical calculations obtained by Garradd and others poured into NASA's Sentry system, which is stationed here, in the Pasadena, California, Jet Propulsion Laboratory (JPL). Sentry is a massive computer that estimates asteroid and comet orbits and identifies Near-Earth Objects (NEOs) that might approach or even destroy our planet. On December 27, Sentry processed all available data on 2004 MN4's dimensions and used those measurements to track its best-guess path to Earth, estimating that there existed a 2.7 percent chance that it would crash into our world on April 13, 2029.

This percentage of risk for an asteroid impact had never been reported before. The Torino scale, the internationally recognized register for NEO impact threats, abides on a spectrum that spans from zero through ten. A zero rating means that no exceptional hazard exists for any such contact. A ten rating predicts an inescapable impact with high-damage potential. Until 2004 MN4 appeared to Roy Tucker, no object had ever reached higher than level one.

Two days after Christmas 2004, Sentry rated MN4 at level four.

In 2004 I'd already been at JPL for several years. After finishing a PhD at Caltech and completing a postdoc, I'd come on board to assist in the radar observation of minor planets, which required travel to the only two radar telescopes in the world capable of such an enterprise: the Goldstone Observatory in Barstow, California, and the then-still-functioning Arecibo Observatory in Puerto Rico.

Goldstone and Arecibo captured images by mapping an asteroid's structure, dimensions, and spin, and this data allows us to evaluate the potential menace the body poses as it hurtles our way. A radar scientist who obtains a space object's impressions does so by cultivating a skill set that combines the precise and patient aesthetics of a daguerreotypist with the hypervigilance of a frightened mother. Perhaps due to these qualifications, the profession attracts a cult of melancholy and paranoid soothsayers who possess the abstract humor I've tried to maintain at JPL and have been refining since my early childhood in Boyle Heights, a small, once-primarily Latino neighborhood in Los Angeles.

I'll admit that I don't appear to possess a classic background for the high sciences or space exploration, especially when you consider the circumstances of my birth and my childhood poverty. Still, a brief review of the leaders of my field reveals that

many of the men and women who disclosed the few known se-
crets of the universe didn't themselves hail from easy circumstances. Isaac Newton, it's been said, was a stunted half-orphan
who so hated his stepfather that he threatened to set fire to his
house and later labored to become a scientific mastermind in
order to wreak vengeance on a schoolyard bully. In the nine-
teenth century, astronomer Caroline Lucretia Herschel's childhood exposure to typhus shrank her such that she grew only a
little over four feet, leaving her in an unmarriageable state that
gave her the liberty to become the first woman to spot a comet.

Compared with these obstacles, my own seem very modest.
Instead of pyromania or typhus, hooligans or bigotry, my am-
bition to escape my mother's stories guided me to the stars. Isabella Juana Valeria De León emerged from her own madre's
womb a vivacious ranconteuse, but her tales as often as not left
me with the foreboding that life on earth amounted to an un-
avoidable catastrophe.

She was born into a tribe of pragmatists who made up the
fishing community of Chicxulub Pueblo in Yucatán. The De
Leóns angled in the ocean that frothed at the village's coastline,
which had collapsed eons earlier into a fathomless crater when
a meteorite struck. The water's sucking, greedy maw stole my
mother's father, her grandmother, two of her uncles, and her
brother, until so few De Leóns survived that the family could
barely feed itself.

My grandmother, Valeria Mercado, determined to save her
daughter by sending her off to waitress in a nearby resort, despite
the girl's perilous beauty and troubling habit of painting bizarre
floral still lifes. Isabella was forced to funnel her talents into the
courtesan's craft, which included schooling her body in illusions,
so she didn't so much walk the hazardous circuit of the hotel's
saloon as offer her breasts and bottom to onlookers via a tantaliz-
ing semaphore. In short order, Valeria entered negotiations with

an inebriated businessman named George Vincent Brooks, who manifested one day at the family home, louche and wild-haired, his negligently manicured hand holding a perfect red rose as he greeted his new fiancée with an unsteady bow. George Vincent Brooks's three names, along with his DNA, today are the only paternal data that I retain, as my mother reacted to her Yanqui groom and a positive pregnancy test by snatching up her peculiar watercolors and fleeing across the border to escape his unhappy habit of wife battery.

After my mother told me about Brother Death, I coped with the warning contained in her story by watching the skies. Within the constellations, I'd see a few dim stars simmering through the smog. I imagined Brother Death plunging through infinity like a tidal wave until he hit the planet and drowned it with his cruelty and terror. The sensations this phantasm produced surged within me like a hereditary sickness, but I tried to dispel my mother's fairy stories by seeing the heavens clearly, with my own eyes. I took in those shimmering plains, which were surrounded by silence and uncrowded by anxiety. There were no demons there, I told myself, only mathematics and mystery.

These private ceremonies developed into a fascination with space. On weekends, I sat in the local library, wearing thick plastic glasses and racking up fines as I scribbled in a series of increasingly dense books. The treatises explained that our world wasn't a nightmare created by Sister Night and her Brothers Fire and Death; it exists as a nearly spherical astronomical object that pirouettes in a solar system also populated by Venus, Mercury, scarlet Mars, the titans Jupiter and Saturn, the ice mammoths Uranus and Neptune, and the lumpy cosmic anklet known as the asteroid belt. As the years swam by, these distractions loosened the grip of my mother's fabulism so I managed to corral Brother Death, shunting him to a far corner of my mind. This left me free to cram into myself a kingdom of ideas, an exalted state of affairs that allowed me to neglect duties like showering, noticing stoplights, eating, and sleeping. While my mother chased me down the hall with a hairbrush or perfected her blasphemies as I drove her in erratic zigzags to the supermarket, I pondered the splendor of the heavens. I contemplated the pink, orange, and iris-blue Cat's Eye nebula, which births radiant colors as it slowly dies. I swooned over the invisible dark matter that holds the spiral galaxies together like the embrace of a mater dolorosa. I meditated over Andromeda's lustrous ring of fire that clutches a cradle of baby stars, which, in turn, encircles a black hole.

I'd never have given a second thought to the frankly unlovely asteroid if it hadn't been for a man in my cosmochemistry seminar, whom I encountered examining pictures of bumpy rocks while we waited for class to begin on a hot fall day in my first year of college. The photos, he explained, showed samples of black basalt recently extracted from the Vredefort Dome, which lies just over a day's walk from his hometown of Frankfort in the Free State province of South Africa. Paul Mthembu was a tall and shining-eyed scientist who inherited his scholarly enthusiasms from his now-deceased parents, who had both been mathematics teachers of genius. At twelve years old, he'd read through Descartes's *Principia Philosophiae* and begun to puzzle through the third volume of Lagrange's *Miscellanea Taurinensia*, a course of study that later diverted from classical mechanics to astrophysics and exogeology upon the violent death of his father, in 1985. Even when he reached the age when most young men spend their days romancing boys or girls, Paul preferred to take melancholy hikes across the grassveld toward the North West province's border. There, he conducted fledgling digs in Vredefort's famous half-circle of hills, which sprang up from the earth after a titanic rock smashed into the planet's crust and transformed it into a lake of lava.

"A meteorite once landed in central South Africa with the force of millions of nuclear bombs," Paul told me in his warm, slightly warbly, voice on our first date at Pasadena's Dog Haus Biergarten, which served a meager brand of boerewors sausage that couldn't compare to the delicacy he remembered from home. "Not much is known of the region before fifty million years ago, when the bubbles in the crust had long cooled into basalt, and the red grasses of the veld first raised their spears to the sky. I think the early peoples were lured to the region by its overlook, as the collision left our land not only glittering with black stones but also graced with a fairy ring."

"Is sounds nice," I said.

He reached out and gently rubbed his thumb on my wrist. "There were many days during my childhood when, after my father—died, I would make the journey from Frankfort to Vredefort, beginning at dusk and reaching the hills the next night. On those evenings, when the moon shone down upon the hills, I thought nothing in the world could be as beautiful. Though I must admit that now, looking at you, Laura, I find myself quite corrected, my dear."

I attempted to answer this with some sort of witticism but only became flustered and almost knocked over a glass of water.

Paul and I spent the first days of our courtship reading chastely together beneath Caltech's olive trees, but we could barely decipher our texts from the interruptions of certain security guards who balked at someone of his complexion taking up space on campus—and the frantic thudding of our hearts. Before long, we fell into each other's arms and from there commenced a series of rigorous experiments. Without these studies in physical science, would I ever have discovered that I'm partial to the sort of long, slow kiss that begins with a soft brush on the eyes and culminates in a burst of chemistry and color around the hips? Paul's hands were large and cold, and surprisingly strong, as he seemed capable of disobeying the laws of gravitation when in a state of ecstasy. I pounced on him, my hair wild, laughing loudly enough that his neuroscience and electrical engineering neighbors pounded on the door, while Paul's eyes sparkled with a capacity for affection so intense that it qualified as a kind of rare intelligence. He kept his gaze fixed on me throughout the act of love, and I stared back, happily fanatical. Afterward, we'd talk— about our childhoods, the sad stories of our parents, the cryptic significance of black basalt, and also about asteroids, into whose cult Paul attempted to seduce me.

I'll admit that I didn't yet consider myself an authentic asteroid person. I entered the field as an agonistic, quietly focusing on radar studies, and only Paul's intensity pulled me toward a study of the minor planets. While I twined my legs around his with the agility of a wrestler, he tried to explain to me how asteroids circulate in the solar system's belt. Those closest to the sun are made of carbon, he rhapsodized, those farthest away are made of silicate rock, while those in the middle of the girdle are metallic, sometimes formed out of incandescent and nearly pure gold . . . the same substance that would, in time, make up my engagement ring. Paul ordered this symbol of fidelity and eternity from a local jeweler in the fifth year of our PhD program, when our by-then-nine-year record of raucous sex and sympathetic research convinced him that he couldn't "live without" me. He presented the gift in a conversation devoid of asteroid references yet still fulfilled in a state of great excitement, while he bent his knee outside the university's Cahill Center for Astronomy and Astrophysics.

"I love you, I love you, I love you, I love you!" we both said.

We married in Boyle Heights in 2001. I began my new job at JPL's prodigy-crammed campus that March. My initiation included an extensive training rotation, where I learned how to map space's surprisingly high sum of potentially hazardous objects under the tutelage of Dr. Somnang Vong, a Cambodian American Kuiper laureate who taught me the history of huge asteroids that had come within a whisker of liquidating cities. Meanwhile, Paul took up a professorship at UCLA's Earth, Planetary, and Space Sciences, where he began to advance a brilliant if controversial argument that the black basalt scarring Vredefort, as well as vast swaths of the earth's crust, offers unrecognized markers of innumerable meteorite landings.

We were almost perfectly happy. There was work, love, and our exciting plans for the future. Unfortunately, these joys were sometimes dissolved by Paul's ritual subjection to traffic stops, the most terrifying of which occurred in 2003 and began with a police officer's question about a flickering taillight. I can't recall what occurred between Paul extracting his driver's license from his wallet and the bony thump of his body as it slammed against the side of our red Honda. But I have no problem remembering how, from my position in the passenger seat, I saw the white folds of his button-down shirt crumple against the glass window, and the dark holstered gun of the officer who felt his hands up and down Paul's sides. "Stay in the car, Laura, stay in the car," Paul said, almost in the same preoccupied tone that he'd use when wondering out loud, over breakfast, about glitches in his electron microscope. I did as I was told, while staring at the police officer's right hand, which he removed from my husband's flanks to rest on the weapon as he yelled obscenities. White sparks shot across my otherwise blinded mind.

Other alarms also threatened to unsteady the life we were building, including the iridescent horrors of 9/11 and my mother's daily phone calls, when she'd yell about terrorists she'd seen lurking around the local supermarket and at the bank. But as the U.S. committed itself to the unfolding catastrophe in Afghanistan, and the phrase "extreme weather" now described the blazes and floods that increasingly ripped through the states, I managed to fend off the ancestral panic I'd first stifled by looking up at the stars. My husband and I endured as the same strong pups who had, I reminded myself, fornicated so hard we'd broken the peace of mind of his dorm-room neighbors. Paul's cold hands still wrangled me while I threw my head back and laughed, my hair streaming; I remained the girl with the long plump thighs that could crush him like a vise. Or nearly.

In the fall of 2004, a few months after Roy A. Tucker first spied 2004 MN4, I realized that Paul didn't look right. His brown cheeks developed a dull sheen, and he complained that his legs felt sore. I told him to build rest periods into his demanding schedule and cooked him soothing soups while trying to amuse him with small talk about problems that Somnang and I had with the klystron tubes at Goldstone, or difficulties with obtaining federal funding for repairs at Arecibo, or some other nonsense.

One night, when he seemed a bit better, I took a long bath and put on a soft robe. I poured us glasses of red wine. Paul sat on our bed without talking, his old, blue T-shirt looking too large and the bones in his face newly visible. I bent forward and kissed him in that soft, brushing way that we both liked. "I love you," he said, seriously. I nudged my hands beneath his clothes. He pushed them away but kissed me harder. I clambered on top of him, moving carefully, since our lovemaking required more delicacy than usual. When we finally clung together, he stared at me, but in a different way. His eyes punched into mine. He grasped and clutched onto my breasts as if he were falling.

"You are my greatest love," he said, afterwards, his voice rasping. "You're the only thing that matters in my life."

I froze. "What's wrong?"

"Nothing."

"Paul, what's going on?"

He turned away from me. I saw that his torso bent in a stiff position. I touched his hips and looked at him.

"It's fine." He closed his eyes. "I've been to the doctor. I'll get some lab results tomorrow. It—it—it shouldn't be any problem."

"You didn't tell me?"

"I didn't want to worry you." He took a deep, shaking breath. "Everything will be all right."

But everything would not be all right. The reason for this new disaster had nothing to do with overwork, the news, or the other hazards that my mother had so diligently trained me to fear. This emergency leapt out at us like a shot in the dark: high-risk colon cancer.

From the moment I learned of my husband's illness, eight weeks passed in a blur. The days melted away and resolved into December 27.

I sat by Paul's hospital bed while he lay in a drugged sleep. His angular head looked like a pencil sketch as it sunk into the white pillow. I hadn't slept more than four straight hours a night for the past month and fought off nausea, as well as a strangely jumpy feeling in my blood. I leaned back in my chair while holding Paul's hand, waiting for my mother to show up so that I could drive to work to get insurance papers. I pressed my mouth against my wrist as the hospital's many vivid odors thickened the air and nearly suffocated me.

"Laura." My mother entered the room and put her hand on Paul's blanketed knee. Her large brown eyes brightened with tears. "Aw, honey, you're as green as a pickle, what the hell."

"Will you just stay here with him for a little while?"

"Laura, listen to me, your face is so thin."

I put my hand to my mouth and covered my nose. "I can't eat anything."

She ran her hand down my arm. "What do you mean, you're not eating? You have to eat. Eat something."

"It's the stress."

Mom lifted her chin and sniffed at me, then went silent for a second. "Your stomach feels bad? You want to puke?"

"Can you not talk about it?"

"Things smell weird?"

"Ah, God."

She hesitated. "'Cause you're not pregnant, right? Because if you're knocked up, you can't be sitting here for hours crying and starving yourself and not getting any healthy circulation and so maybe screwing up the baby."

"Mom, please, I have to go."

I touched Paul's cheek with my lips and almost ran through the hospital's stinking halls. Hugging myself, I fast-walked outside, toward the parking lot, and jammed my key into my car door. I drove the route to JPL. The trees flashed past. The world was drained of color. At a stoplight, my body thrilled with a nasty thudding sensation. I gripped the wheel and tried to remember if my menstrual cycle had been normal for the past two months, but all I could retrieve were frantic episodes in oncologists' offices and my own pointless rage at medical bureaucracy.

I wound my way through JPL's beige campus until I reached the parking lot of the Center for Near-Earth Object Studies, which held a smattering of cars despite the holidays. I presented my badge and entered the foyer. It was empty. I took the elevator to the fourth floor and stepped out into a hallway unexpectedly antic with gesticulating, messy-haired aerospace engineers and astrophysicists. In my office, I grabbed my folder of papers, and when I came back out, a young, thickly bearded radar astronomer named Advay exited my boss's door with his arms full of binders and his cheeks gone glossy with excitement. Advay ran down the corridor toward a scrum of arguing scientists. I looked in and saw the thin and balding figure of Somnang squinting at the five monitors that he'd set up on three desks. He typed quickly but raised his head when he sensed me there.

"You've heard," he said.

"What's happening?" I asked.

"Oh. I see, you haven't. We're just having an unpleasant bit of excitement." Somnang blinked his dark eyes at me. "2004 MN4."

I gripped my forehead, trying to think. "The rock they found at Kitt Peak?"

"Yes. But don't you mind any of that now. How is Paul, Laura? I'm sorry I've been out of touch."

"He's . . ." I swallowed. "What's going on with MN4?"

Somnang regarded me for a moment. "Just getting some new data, nothing for you to worry about."

"Nothing to worry about?"

He shrugged, looking exhausted. "The Torino's been raised to four."

"Right," I said, after a long pause.

"Numbers in from Australia make it look quite interesting."

"Interesting."

"A one in thirty-seven chance it might hit here in 2029."

I touched my stomach. "Isn't it huge?"

"Yes, it does seem that way."

"If it hit, the impact would be like one hundred thousand Hiroshimas. Do I remember that right?"

Somnang's phone rang, and he widened his eyes in a bemused expression of horror. "I suppose that's why some ghastly newsperson keeps ringing me every two minutes."

He took the call. I stayed in the doorway for a couple seconds, my lips moving as I made silent calculations, and then left.

I wove through the hallway's sweaty huddle of my mostly male colleagues, who waved charitable greetings at me while barking risk assessments to each other. I took the elevator down. I exited the building. I held my folder to my chest and walked rapidly to my brown Volvo. I tried to put my key in the door's lock but fumbled it, and my key ring fell to the ground. The asphalt rushed up to meet me as I sat down hard, scattering my papers. I curled over. Gripping my stomach with both hands, I looked up.

Anyone else would have seen only a blue sky filled with thin white clouds. But beyond the eye-swallowing sun, I made out the far-off shadow of Brother Death, the same demon I'd stopped fearing so many years before. I imagined him sailing down at us through a vertical ocean of dark matter, his thick and flailing body shedding lightning storms and gravitational waves that tore open the atmosphere with neon-red explosions. Even while I'd done everything I could to convince myself he wasn't real—studying physics, becoming a scientist, marrying Paul—Brother Death had been plummeting toward us all this time. He plunged headfirst, his unspeakable face aiming to crush my world into broad lakes of lava, while a stream of irrevocable curses flowed from his cold, stone mouth.

Roy Tucker, David Tholen, and Fabrizio Bernardi seem to have nourished some of the same amazed anxieties about MN4 that I did in JPL's parking lot, if the name they chose for their asteroid gives us any clue: On July 19, 2005, they christened the rock Apophis. Apophis was the Egyptian lord of chaos who took the form of a giant serpent that lurked in the underworld, circling his tail around the earth and making the mountains shake with his roar. Ra, the falcon-headed sun deity, is said to have birthed Apophis from his sparkling womb, but Apophis didn't love Ra or anything else except for his own lust for pure destruction. After spending centuries perfecting a plot for how to snuff out all life, Apophis attacked his father with his basilisk stare. The sun god almost lost the fight. But Ra knew that if he died, so would humanity, as well as every shining being in heaven and every foul thing that crept in hell. So Ra transformed into a mighty cat and slew Apophis with his adamantine claws, ripping the snake into shreds.

For three days in December of 2004, it looked like Apophis was well on course to crush our planet in twenty-four years unless Ra or some other monumental force deflected it. Still, world governments couldn't respond to the asteroid because a catastrophe nearly as great had already arrived: An Indian Ocean earthquake had devastated Sumatra on December 26, sending forth a tsunami that killed over 230,000 people in Indonesia, India, Thailand, Sri Lanka, and other countries. In that last grim week of December, armies and aid agencies marshaled their services, while a menacing shadow hung over the globe.

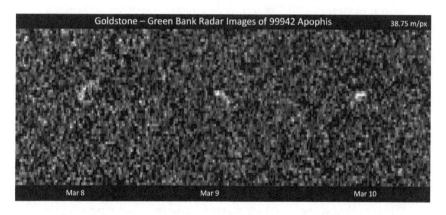

And then, as fast as it had appeared in space, Apophis just as quickly transformed back into a harmless stone in the sky. In the final hours of December 27, astronomers discovered archival images of Apophis taken on March 15. These pictures allowed for a recalculation of Apophis's 2029 orbit. The new numbers revealed that the asteroid actually possessed a miniscule chance of hitting Earth that year. Planetary scientists eventually downgraded Apophis's Torino scale level to zero.

Of course, I didn't know about the fate of Apophis as I sat in the JPL's parking lot crying about my husband and my unborn baby on that December morning. I understood only that I had to find a way to defend my family from Brother Death. I couldn't cure disease, war, hate, or the other forms of violence that might invade our lives without warning. But I had at least one skill. From that point on, I didn't feel antagonistic toward my vocation. I became a zealous asteroid researcher.

It's now sixteen years later, Sunday, September 6, 2020; 1 PM in Pasadena. I'm sitting at our kitchen table, which has, for the moment, become my de facto workstation. Here, I'm supposed to be drafting part of a congressional proposal for how to address asteroid threats, a project that promises my advancement from planetary scientist into policymaker. I've been authorized to write the history section of a huge, multi-author project called the *National Near-Earth Object Preparedness Strategy and Action Plan*. But I'm not working on my part of the report. I'm staring out the window because the stress of the present moment has triggered memories of other tough times, like Paul's cancer, my mother's stories of her punishing childhood, and the difficult circumstances of my first and only pregnancy.

Outside, smoke from a nearby inferno and recent firework-lit protests soars over houses and winds around telephone poles. The explosive Bobcat Fire started early this morning when a power line malfunctioned somewhere around Sierra Madre, about seven miles from here. And since Derek Chauvin murdered George Floyd in May, activists have set off Black Cats, ground spinners, and star-filled Roman Candles every night. The late-summer heat prickles my skin despite our air conditioner, and the sky dulls with ash, creating a mirage of snow floating above the trees. A bizarre, orange sun gleams through the haze. The smoke's particulate matter wafts into the house, settling on our food, the kitchen table, my pencils, my green notebook, and my computer. I rub my stinging eyes and force myself to turn back to work.

On my screen shines a black-and-white collage of photos and documents saved in a file I've titled *A History of Hazardous Objects*. The papers give accounts of the large asteroids that have either threatened to hit or have actually struck the planet. Beyond Tucker's Apophis, these objects include a gigantic fireball that exploded over eastern Siberia's Podkamennaya Tunguska River in 1908, injuring horrified Evenki villagers and drawing the attention of Russian mineralogist Leonid Kulik; the colossal meteorite that smashed into my mother's hometown of Chicxulub sixty-six million years ago with so much force that it killed all dinosaurs on the planet, according to the physicist Luis Alvarez; the great cosmic boulders that pummeled the early solar system, leading geologist Gerald Wasserburg to propose the hypothesis of a Late Heavy Bombardment; and the nine-pound rock that bashed through the roof of a homemaker named Ann Hodges in eastern Alabama in 1954, leaving a bruise the size of a small tombstone on her lower body and a trauma so great that she descended into mental illness.

"Mom?"

My son, Tomás, appears in the hallway. He wears jeans the color of lake water on his long, thin legs. His faded-to-gray shirt bags across his narrow chest. He smiles at me with half his mouth, so my pulse hiccups. He looks just like his father did when I first met him. Sixteen years old.

"What's going on?" I ask.

Tomás stuffs his hands in his pockets. "Grandma wants a big glass of red wine and some mint Milanos."

"It's too early to drink, and she finished the cookies already." I click out of the file and turn around. "You hungry?"

He raises his eyebrows with interest.

"A sandwich, maybe?"

"All right."

I open the fridge and grab packages of pink ham, pale lettuce. Tomatoes. Out comes a loaf of bread from the cupboard. I assemble a stack, with green leaves fluttering from the bread slices. Tomás comes up behind me and puts his head on my shoulder as I tear off a paper towel and fold it around the sandwich's bottom half. He hums a little, a song I don't know.

"I'm going out later," he tells me, casually.

"Where?"

"Just getting a few people together."

"What, a protest?"

He shrugs. "Mmm. Something."

"Let's wait and see if we can go with you." I give him his sandwich, kiss him quickly on his cheek. "Remember what I said."

"I'm not going to get sick," he says impatiently. "I'll wear a mask."

"That's not all I'm worried about."

I watch his jaw working. His long, slim hands grasp the bread. It feels like his body is my body, and my body is his body, but I know that's not true at all.

"I can't be here all the time," he says, not looking at me.

"For right now, please just do your homework."

"I did."

"You know I mean the problems I gave you."

I touch my son's hardening face. Before he can complain, I exit the kitchen, pad through the hall, and make my way to the TV room that sits at the back of the house. My mother sits in a soft chintz chair in front of the television, which she's turned on and muted. She's watching a reality show starring angry, large-bosomed women who spend a lot of time crying loudly into their drained wine glasses. Mom's cheeks are flushed pink, and her hair looks as if it's been tinted to resemble a black-and-white cookie.

Mom colored her roots devotedly until 2018. That was when we all agreed she should move to an expensive and highly monitored senior community because of a broken left leg caused less by a stumble in her apartment's bathroom than her early-onset and severe osteoporosis. Once Paul and I installed her in the Golden Breezes Assisted Living Facility, which is only two miles away from our house, she discontinued all hair upkeep; she also stopped laughing, yelling at me, telling me scary stories, or painting her eyes with their customary filigree of kohl. I tried to attribute this change to her graceful embrace of the aging process and not to any trouble adjusting to her new situation. This hypothesis has since been deeply refuted: Her complexion, attitude, and verbosity have improved approximately 500 percent now that a plague rages across the land with such morbid force that Paul and I yanked her from that COVID-infested place four months ago and brought her to live here. But her hair remains bifurcated between the ebony ends and her silvered skull, which she fusses over but still won't do anything about.

"Mom," I say.

She darts her eyes at me. "Bringing me wine? Milanos? Oh, I see: No."

"It's eleven o'clock in the morning."

She points to the screen. "The girls do it, it's fun."

"Drinking and sugar are bad for your blood pressure."

"I like being bad. I always wanted to be super bad. Now that you have all the responsibility, I'm going to be terrible. I'm so happy."

"Mom."

"Okay, you're right. The kid shouldn't see me hitting the sauce so early. Bring it to me in a thermos."

"Do you want some real food?"

"Did you know I was a millionaire's girlfriend when I first got to the states? He used to take me to the Ritz, where he'd make me do a lot of sex things until I smacked him across the face with a lamp. It was better than working in that goddamned cafeteria, though. And maybe he was a bastard, but not so bad as you-know-who."

"I can make you a ham sandwich."

Her face is illuminated by dingy light streaming in through a window that looks out onto our half-dead, normally sunny yard. "I'm glad you're a good, good person. Look at you, with a man and a baby and everything and your science stuff."

I squat in front of her, touching her knees. "Tomás isn't a baby anymore."

She grabs both sides of my face and kisses my cheeks. "*You* are my baby. My *baby*. Yes, you are."

"Yes."

She presses her forehead to mine and smiles. Her eyes fill with tears.

"You know, I never told you anything," she says.

"Mom, you've told me. I know."

"Remember the story about the zombie husband?"

"That was a good one."

"Yeah, it's best I never said anything to you, really. What happened to me with that man, and then with this country."

"It's okay. Everything's all right. Do you want anything to eat?"

"Maybe later."

I rest my cheek on her thigh. Mom plays with my hair while explaining that if I'm not careful I'll start looking ratty because I could use a nice tidy cut with lots of layers. We stay like this until we hear a thunking noise coming from the office.

"I'll be back," I say.

I transit the hallway to the next room over. The door's closed, but from within I can make out a *pap pap pap* sound.

"Damn. Damn."

When I enter, I see the flurry of an arm. The flash of an eye.

It's Paul. He jostles a drawer in his metal filing cabinet, which sits between his large oak table and my newly installed walnut desk, lugged over from my former office. He sweats over the stuck drawer, but when he sees me come in, he starts laughing.

"Don't try to help!" he gasps.

His face is lean and shining. His bones etch his forearms more than they used to. His neck is thinner, his hair is going gray. He's still my Paul, but years of treatments have marked him, and the boy I knew is gone.

I go to the cabinet and fiddle with the handle of the drawer. It pops open.

He grins at me.

"You're welcome."

He sits down and pulls me into his lap. "Did I tell you about the findings in the Tanzania basalt bed?"

"The shocked quartz? Yes."

"I think people will find it very convincing."

"About the basalt."

"Shocked quartz is a classic sign of craters. It's a confirmation of the connection!"

"Yes!"

After his diagnosis in 2004, Paul had three surgeries. Then eight rounds of chemotherapy. We gritted through another tough year when his treatments weakened him until he couldn't care for himself. Paul took up residence in our bedroom, mostly lying on his "better" side so that he could hold our fat, giggling, infant son while one-handedly tapping at his keyboard as he wrote yet another article. Since then, he's been in remission three times, for as long as nine years once. And he's been in remission now for two years, a state of affairs that I hope to God the doctor will tell us hasn't changed. We'll be learning that news this coming Wednesday, which is the date for his three-month checkup.

I snuggle into my husband's chest while he tells me about Tanzania. Paul's idea that Earth's many regions of common basalt bedrock are proof of millions of prior meteorite landings still hasn't been accepted universally by the academy. His bid for tenure at UCLA proved—how can I say this—disappointing. Only a spate of peripheral, mid-2000s work on left-handed amino acids in Tagish Lake meteorites earned him enough votes for a lectureship. But I've learned that Paul's not a person who can be stopped by trivialities like group consensus or by much of anything else. That's why, instead of wandering randomly around the house in a state of sluggish panic over the virus and the fires (like I am), he now starts digging into his files and pulling out a study on a new basalt bed found near the Vredefort Dome. He sits down at his desk and glares at a computer screen fizzing with all-capped text.

"If I could just . . ." he mumbles.

His eyes shadow over. I can see the polluted sky outside the window and, even though the whole house is shut tight, I faintly smell the smoke from the fire and the firework vapor.

I leave, closing the door behind me. On the walls of this hallway hang a few of the framed watercolor curlicues my mother made as a girl, before George Vincent Brooks put an end to her art. She calls these works "roses," though they don't resemble flowers at all. One of the pictures, I see, has disappeared, leaving a bare rectangle. *That's weird, where is it? In the living room?* I go in there . . . no. *In the bathroom or garage?* No. I meander through the laundry room, the kitchen, and the second bathroom, finally finding the painting in my mother's bedroom, that is, in my old office. It's a black-and-white outline of oblongs and circles, like an intertwined series of eights or infinity signs mingled with spirals and secret codes. She's put it on her bureau, by her vanity mirror, so she can see it when she wakes. I wipe off specks of dust from the picture frame, then glimpse my face in the mirror's reflection. The skin of my jaw hangs in a new way; I look a lot older than I did last year.

I leave my mother's bedroom and stand in the living room. I breathe in, then out, in, then out, in a manner I hope resembles the meditation method my gynecologist told me about the last time I saw her. Staring at the sofa cushions and the Berber rug, I don't know what to do with myself. I can hear Tomás on the phone. I know he's talking to Cecil because of the fury in his voice, though I can't tell whether the objects of his complaints are the police or his parents.

"They can't do this," my son says. "They can't do this anymore, we won't let them."

I return to the kitchen and sit back down at the table. Opening my computer back up to *A History of Hazardous Objects,* I look at my documents on Tunguska, Chicxulub, the Bombardment, and eastern Alabama. My green notebook's full of lists and graphs, but I haven't even written a topic sentence.

Congress ordered NASA to compile the action plan two years ago, after an asteroid as tall as the Trump Building on Wall Street sailed within 1.4 million klicks of Earth on March 7, 2018, triggering a brief, high-ranking frenzy; an asteroid that size can annihilate a large city, and 1.4 million kilometers isn't far in space terms. If the government stays serious about detecting and neutralizing these giant rocks, our report might finally persuade it to launch a satellite capable of rerouting asteroids with projectiles or blasting them with nuclear warheads. That mission would require a surveillance craft to execute a specific set of orbits, the type that we've already designed for other minor-planet observation missions. In order to canvass the solar system with sufficient breadth to spot rogue asteroids, the vehicle would have to circumnavigate the earth in a series of oblongs, or half-circles, which space engineers also describe as petals.

I grab a pen and add a sketch to my notebook.

2
The God of Thunder

Hours before dawn, Paul wakes me with a kiss on the shoulder. I look over at the clock. Three AM. He's spent the night in his/our study, struggling over a paper.

"Laura." He lifts his lips from my skin. A tin-colored street light fights through the smoke outside. Even at this hour it's still hot, and the air settles thickly on my limbs.

"Are you okay?"

He doesn't answer.

"Paul?"

"I've just been thinking of back home."

I rest my cheek on his chest and wait.

"When I was seven years old," he says, "my dad took me to the dome for the first time." Paul pauses. "Or have I told you this story before?"

"Tell it to me anyway."

"Well, you know how beautiful it is, from when you and I went there before. The sun on the grass. The Vaal like a white ribbon threading through."

"It's a great place."

"He and I sat on the southeastern side, with a view of the farmlands. Old Hattingsrust farmed sorghum there, and we knew Enkelbosch for his maize. I looked down at the stones beneath us. It's hard country for crops because impacts and old lava flows left deposits in the soil. When I looked around, I saw black rocks everywhere. My father said they were an ancient form of basalt, something I remembered for the rest of my life."

As my husband talks, I can hear the sharp, popping sounds of the fireworks outside, the blare of car horns, and people chanting.

"He told me about a myth he'd heard when he was a boy. 'Old folks say that a long time ago, an angel flew down to Vredefort. Before then, there'd been no earth, only fire. But when the angel's foot touched that spot, the world was born. Those black rocks mark all his footprints.' While my dad explained this to me, he reached down and picked up a shard of basalt that lay on the ground. He gave it to me so that I could touch it, grow familiar with it.

"'People tell this story, Paul,' he said, 'but it's just a superstition. Even more important than if there are angels and spirits, or how life began and why, there's something else you must understand: This is *your* country. Your great-grandfather was born here, your grandfather was born here, I was born here, and you were born here. It's yours by right. There are people living here now who could look at this field and not notice the marks of your ancestors. They'd see only their own fantasies in it. That we don't belong here. That they bring us order instead of destruction. But don't look with their eyes. Even when they try to force you.'"

Paul stops talking. We lie there for a long time. I know not to speak.

Paul kisses me again, softly, on my temple.

"The work I do is for him," he says.

September 8.

Breakfast. Smoke lounges thicker in the air outside, gray and poisonous. None of us mentions this as we take our places at the kitchen table. Paul and I have cooked egg white scrambles with broccoli and black beans, although he can't eat any solid food because of tomorrow's checkup. A pot of green salsa sits on the table alongside a carafe of coffee and a bottle of olive oil. I pile my mother's plate with the food. She waves a fork over her proteins as if trying to magic them into a cinnamon bun. Her two-tone hair twirls up in a chignon, and thin, intricate calligraphies of black eyeliner have made their reappearance. I purse my mouth as if to say, *not bad.* She laughs while scoffing at the food. *I know,* she thinks at me, *but where's my bacon and champagne? Eat your eggs, lady,* I think back at her. She dramatically sighs while Paul sits next to Tomás, neither of them noticing the change in her appearance. Both of them scuff the screens of their gadgets with their thumbs and shake their heads.

"He can't win," Tomás says. "Not after everything we've been through."

"It could happen, son." Paul puts his iPad beneath his chair. "Don't be too disappointed if it does."

"Are you kidding? Cecil and I'll go crazy."

My mother grooms her eyebrows with her pinkies. "You think this guy is bad? Bad is when you get your ass dragged from your bed in the middle of the night by drug goons who chop off your head and leave you in the desert, and nothing can happen because the president is on their payroll."

"That's not going to happen here, Mom," I say.

"Maybe," she answers.

"He's a fascist!" Tomás says.

"There's nothing you can do about it right now," Paul says, "except not let him run your life."

Tomás grimaces. "He's already running our lives. That's why we're going downtown tomorrow. We're setting off fireworks and marching."

"You're not going to play with any kind of explosives, and your dad and I can't go with you tomorrow, anyway," I say.

"Then I'll go with Grandma, and we'll meet Cecil there."

"Yeah, I want to go to protests," my mother says. "I want to scream at people."

"No," I say. "We'll all go to together sometime next week."

"But I told him I'd meet him at eleven o'clock."

I emphasize my words by jabbing my knife into my scramble. "Not alone."

"But Cec and I will be together, so safely, and all distanced." Tomás looks over at his father. "Dad, come on."

"I don't think so." Paul takes a sip of water, then sets down his glass. "I don't know."

"But we're so careful," Tomás says. "Just, like, not even touching. Not even breathing."

"The police are more dangerous to you than COVID," Paul says.

"Animals," my mother says. "What I saw on TV, with the bullets and the hoses? We should dig a hole in the ground and fill it with wild dogs and throw in all those jackasses."

"Right?" Tomás says.

"Please, Mom." I grasp Tomás's hand. "I don't want you to go to a place where there are crowds and law enforcement and probably lots of corona unless I'm sure that you're safe."

"Well, a lot of people want a lot of things. A lot of people want there not to be fucking executions and, like, modern lynchings in this country."

"Hey!" Paul says.

"And you can't know if Cecil is infectious," I say.

"He's not infectious." Tomás's neck and cheeks turn a deeper shade. "He's perfect."

"That's not a diagnosis."

Tomás turns to his father. "You should come with us."

"Apologize to your mom for your language."

"I'm sorry."

Paul and I look at each other. I shake my head.

"I'll go with you tomorrow night," Paul says. "But as soon as there's any trouble, we're gone."

Tomás's smile makes him look exactly like he did when he was five years old.

"Honey, you can't," I tell my husband. "You're going to have to rest up from your test."

Paul frowns at his glass. "It's in the morning, and later I'll be fine."

"No, you won't."

"Ay, the hospital," Mom says. She flutters her hands as if trying to ward off a jinx. "I forgot you had to do that, baby."

Tomás throws back his head and closes his eyes. The rest of us go quiet. I stand and walk toward the sink, rinse out a cup. I glance up to see that pewter smoke crams every window in this room.

"We'll do it another time, then," Paul says. He lets out a long breath.

After breakfast, it's time for me to disinfect the kitchen. Before March of this year, I wasn't much of a housekeeper. I'd slowly wipe a rag across the kitchen counter but wouldn't notice the occasional fleck of tomato spume or broccoli floss. I liked living like that, not really caring about mess because my mind was wizarding up theories about asteroids secreted in the shadows of Jupiter and Mars. Once the pandemic came, though, I lost the disheveled, sapient person I used to be and got replaced by a deranged janitor. And I'm not the only one. I've read of people so afraid of touching the virus that they steep fruit and vegetables in bleach, or poison themselves with hand sanitizer. I've managed to keep myself from that level of mania, but starting in early spring, I began to scour all our food, as well as anything else my family might touch, with harried and destructive scrubs of a wire brush.

Today I pull out a bucket from the broom closet, then pour soap on a sponge. I press out lather onto the cleared table. I rinse and start again. After that, I wipe the sink. The refrigerator. The door handles and the toaster. I wash until the room drips and glitters, and the puddles on the counter fill with flashes beamed down by the overhead lights.

From the TV room, I hear Mom laughing at her show. Tomás said that he'd take care of the bathroom, but he's playing

antisocial music in his bedroom because he can't see his boyfriend tomorrow.

I crouch down and wash the floor, listening to the *tap tap tap*
of a leak beneath the sink and lightly obsessing over a study I
recently read of Wuhan's Huoshenshan Hospital. In July, scientists obtained samples of the virus that lapped through its wards
like the tide. Wearing protective gear, the researchers swabbed
the walls, computer mice, handrails, doorknobs, and floors.
They found that the contagion misted continually from infected
patients and radiated from every single surface. Still, not one
member of the hospital staff contracted COVID, it's not clear why.
The authors of the study sparked worldwide excitement when
they hypothesized that contaminated areas don't present a clear
and present danger, and we don't need to touch our mail with
rubber gloves or compulsively sanitize our homes.

I pour more water on the floor.

Cleaning these days always makes me meditate on the virus's
ingenious architecture. SARS-COV-2 particles are round—like
planets I think, as I move the dripping sponge across the wood
planks. Proteins spike from their sticky spheres, giving them a
rough and alien appearance. When an infected person exhales,
these bodies fly through the air, toward the atmosphere of another person. If carriers are standing far enough away, their contagion only manages a flyby and veers off harmlessly into space.
Another saving grace: Soap disrupts the virus's greasy layer and
so deflects it from the skin. But if a particle manages to achieve
contact, its spike attaches to receptors on a human cell, pene-
trating its membrane and unleashing a detonation that can tear
through an elderly body like my mother's or liquidate a body
with a preexisting condition like Paul's. The virus will erupt like a
crashing meteorite or a wildfire that sets free all the toxins inside
the blood. It'll burst like a mutating cell or the fireworks that

keep skywriting the message that only three and a half months ago, Chauvin's knee crushed down on George Floyd's neck until he choked to death.

I push the sponge into a dusty corner, scrubbing harder and harder and harder.

My hands are raw when I finally rise from the floor, sweating. The smoke pushes its face against all sides of our house while Tomás's agro music beats from his room. The kitchen shines like a knife. I squeeze my eyes shut and try to breathe while listening to the leak. Tomorrow is my husband's quarterly checkup for colorectal adenocarcinoma. Too much is happening at once.

"Everything's going to be fine," Paul says, through his mask. It's the next day, and we're at the hospital at 8 AM in the morning.

"Yes," I say.

"Write your report."

"I will." I clutch my briefcase to my stomach.

"I'll go find us a cup of coffee." He stands up and walks away from the bench in the hallway where the orderly placed us, spaced far apart from the few other patients who've arrived at this hour for tests or surgery.

We're at USC's Norris Cancer Center in downtown Los Angeles. In good years, we have a standing appointment every three months, and in bad years, we make the drive here almost every day. This is a good year, at least medically speaking, I remind myself as I try to straighten my back instead of slumping in my seat. Staff, wreathed in wrinkled plastic so they look like mistakes made by a 3D printer, walk to and fro. I know some of the guards by name and many of the nurses, though today everyone looks indistinguishable behind their masks. Typically, we begin the day in the small Blood Draw anteroom, crammed together with other unblinking and disassociating patients. This morning the hospital is at half, or even a third, of capacity. I stare at the wall opposite me. A large oil painting of two indistinct human figures holding hands and walking toward a burst of dark-gold light, which I have never seen before and don't like, offers the only relief from the space's implacable brightness.

"They took the coffee away," Paul says, wandering back up with his hands in his pockets. "I guess they don't want anyone to touch anything."

"You can't drink right now anyway."

"I know." He sits next to me and puts his hand on my thigh.

"I love you," I say.

"Write your report."

"I want to be with you."

"You are with me."

"Be with you completely. Without distraction."

"Darling. It's routine."

A swathed nurse walks up. I recognize her square black glasses. "Hey, Paul," she says.

We've known this woman for years. She has dark hair, a large smile, and a twelve- or thirteen-year-old-son named Colin. "Hey, Connie," I say.

My husband grins at her behind his mask. "Connie, my girl."

"Crazy times." She shakes her head and laughs.

I gesture at the empty seats in the waiting room. "Where is everyone?"

"Scared away." She shrugs. "How you guys been?"

"Pretty good," Paul says.

Connie holds out her hand to him. "Want to get started?"

Paul leans over and kisses the side of my head. "Write your report."

"I can't concentrate."

"Try."

I watch them walk away. They push a glass-fronted door open and disappear.

I brood at the painting of the couple journeying toward the afterlife. I'll be here for at least four hours. Blood, endoscopy, colonoscopy. Usually my mother comes with me, but the new rules won't allow two guests. I touch my face and find that my mask has slid beneath my nose. I tug it up and take hold of my briefcase. I walk from the hallway toward the chapel, off the hospital's main lobby.

The chapel is cool and hushed. It's empty. I've been here many times. My mother and I first came to this place in 2004, during the days just before Apophis pegged four on the Torino scale, and we waited to hear the results of Paul's initial, nine-hour-long surgery. We'd sat in the back row, and I laid my head on her lap while fighting off the nausea that I didn't yet understand signaled my pregnancy. I pressed my face into her hip and tried to smother my terror by focusing on the 40 percent chance of survival that Paul's doctors had estimated in the event the surgery was successful.

That's how I once prayed in this little hospital church while Mom stroked my sweating scalp with her small, hard hands. Now I'm alone, and I'm here only for the quiet. Blue and pink upholstered benches lead up to a small altar table, which is covered with white lace. Lamps shed gold light into the air. I move to the middle of the room and slide onto a bench before taking out my computer. I place my briefcase on my thighs and my computer on my briefcase. I open my EliteBook. I squint as the screen flashes.

I sign into the hospital internet and scroll through my research on significant meteorite incidents that range from four billion years ago to modern times. There are a lot of examples to draw on, but I decide that today's work will be writing a digest of the Tunguska Event. Leonid Kulik, the Russo-Japanese War hero and scientist, only recorded this early twentieth-century disaster decades after the fact. I place the pads of my fingers on my keyboard and stare into the gloom of the chapel. Eventually, the space fills with the sounds of clicking and tapping as I try to synopsize Kulik's findings, which he made during a clumsy Soviet expedition into the wrecked Russian Far East.

The Tunguska event proves a critical addition to this congressional report as it demonstrates how even a small projectile could wreak widespread casualties. On June 30, 1908, a meteor estimated at 232–656 feet in diameter entered the atmosphere of eastern Siberia at 45,000 mph. There was no direct impact, and the stony body atomized three to six miles above the earth's surface. The bolide sent out a wall of flame and a shock wave that shattered the eastern Siberian taiga, a forest of resin-scented Dahurian larch and pine trees.

Nineteen years later, in 1927, the mineralogists Leonid Kulik and Yevgeny Krinov documented the disaster during their springtime expedition to Russia's Podkamennaya Tunguska River. This campaign was plagued not only by the mischief of Krinov, a master of planetary sciences and an unexpectedly disruptive adjutant, but also by Kulik's own errors, which prevented him from embedding with the region's Evenki people. This community of herders had suffered exploitation, violence, and compelled acculturation from the day the Tsar first enforced taxation of the tribes with Cossack voiskos. But, as these men's leader, Vasily Okhchen, explained to Kulik, not even those depredations prepared them for the morning when the heavens hurled down volcanic rain that flattened the trees and sizzled the shrieking villagers with its otherworldly heat. . . .

The sky broke in two and Ogdy, the thunder god, descended from the clouds in a bright blue flame, Okhchen said in the Russian tongue, his small face peering out from his furs as he turned his Yakut stallion and pointed toward the mountain of dead trees in the distance. Blue and pink fire filled the heavens. We were blinded. Flames burned our skin. Then came the thunder. *Crack, crack, crack. Crack, crack, crack, crack, crack.* Okhchen barked the noises while grasping the reins of his horse. Fire came down and burned our skin. The earth shook as if it feared the blue lord of storms. The forest died, the trees crashed to the earth. The animals perished. Now Ogdy dwells there. Our shaman says that today it is a place where only the thunder god should wander. This is why I say to you that we will lead you no further. Before we reach the deadwood, we must go back.

But is there a crater, and how large is it? Kulik asked, regarding the Indigenous man from his low perch on his sledge. Kulik was muffled in a stinking bear rug and attempted to take notes in his leather book despite the unvanquishable mist on his spectacles. Next to him, Krinov burrowed his massive shoulders beneath their shared fur and shook his head with bemused scorn.

There will be no crater, you poxy fool, Krinov muttered.

The testimony of these brutes amounts to nothing more than codswallop and humbug.

Kulik gestured at the heaps of fallen trees in the far distance. And what would account for the destruction of millions of Siberian pines?

Krinov shrugged. A drought. Wood rot. An earthquake.

The great Yevgeny Krinov hears a tale of fire tumbling from the sky and sees evidence of a shock front on a forest and still rejects my theory?

Do you not think it strange that when, I, the world's expert in meteorites, has explained to you that space stones are as rare as angel farts, you prove incapable of heeding my advice?

Why did you come here but to vex me? Kulik groused, stabbing his fountain pen angrily into his book.

The two Soviets quarreled beneath Okhchen's impassive gaze and within a company of ten horse-mounted and equipment-carrying Evenki men, who all wore the same sable fur and grim expression as their leader. For his part, Krinov was tall and thick, a giant from the Tambov Oblas, whereas Kulik bore weak lungs from his travails on the Yalu River, where he had fought the Japanese decades earlier. Four fawn-brown Yakut stallions drew their sledge, inspired regularly by a long leather lash held by Krinov.

No man has entered the deadwood for twenty years, nyungnyai, Okhchen said. What you ask us to do is forbidden, and we are afraid.

Fear is for weaklings, Krinov said, raising the lash and touching it lightly across Okhchen's leg, so that the guide's horse startled.

Okhchen himself did not flinch. He stared at Krinov and betrayed no emotion. A deadly silence settled over the Indigenous people. Nothing could be heard across the tundra but the wind and the soft nickers of the stallions.

Fear is a great teacher for men who can see their way through it, Okhchen finally said.

Go on, go on, Krinov laughed, rummaging in his furs for a flask.

We will pay you more, Kulik begged. Okhchen, please, do not mind him. We will give you twice your fee if you take us to the place the stone fell. Three times. Four times the fee.

Okhchen spat on the ground. His face remained unyielding. Yet, without a word, he turned his horse east and trotted toward the disaster site. The rest of the Evenki drew up their reins and followed in a stern procession. Krinov, emboldened, struck the sledge-pulling horses, and the adventurers strove past new green growths of larch and the spring's last layers of frost until they reached the perimeter of the crushed forest.

It should be somewhere here, Okhchen, you must point me in the right direction, Kulik said, scrambling out of the sledge. He withdrew his vest pocket camera, and dashed hither and thither through the deadwood while taking photographs of the lifeless trees. The ripped and severed trunks lay on the ground, rotting in the melting ice pack. This sight caused Kulik to flinch as he remembered himself as a young soldier, lifted off his feet by a rushing blast wave and then thrown among the corpses strewn on the bloody Yalu during the war.

As Kulik paled, and the Evenki assembled silently on the forest's perimeter, Krinov clambered over the lumber until he reached a large rock. He leapt onto the stone and squatted upon it. He yanked his fur hat over his eyebrows and commenced sucking on his flask. What are you gawping at, you muskrat in high heels? he roared, laughing.

Kulik rubbed his face with a hasty hand. The crater, it must be here somewhere, he gasped as he stumbled over the snow-clogged tree roots, willing himself to forget his disturbing vision.

We have brought you to this place, Okhchen said. Now it is time to leave.

Okhchen, you must help me look, Kulik wheezed, peering up into a whiteness nearly indistinguishable from the snow cover. Perhaps the meteor did not reach the earth at all, he thought. It might have exploded in the sky. In which case there might be fragments buried beneath the trees. Kulik kicked at the icy drifts on the ground and picked up a shard of gravel. He held it high in the air. Could this be something? he asked.

Yes, nyungnyaki, that is surely what you seek, Okhchen said in a flat voice as the wind gained speed, sleeking the men's furs and sending a chill through their chests.

I do not understand your foreign words, sir, Kulik grunted, as he loaded black stones into his pockets.

I only am calling you and your friend mighty warriors, Okhchen said.

Bollocks, cursed Krinov.

Mighty and terrible warriors whose journey has been victorious. I am sure that you and your ho'kor will be celebrated and honored with wine and women when you return to Moscow with these pebbles. We must depart this instant so as not to anger the god of thunder.

Kulik, are you such an empty-head that you think that rumors of heavenly bodies will be found in those little clods you are diddling? Krinov jeered, carousing on his boulder while drinking his fill.

It is possible that this common-enough-looking rock is evidence of the calamity, Kulik said, clutching his samples and squinting into the rising gale.

And when you smell the sulfur in your wife's burps, do you fear suddenly that you are in the presence of the Great Adversary? Krinov bellowed, while the Evenki, still on their horses, murmured amongst themselves as the wind increased in strength and pressure.

I am sure I do not need to grace your revilements with a response, Kulik huffed, as he extracted a loupe from his pocket and glared at the stony fragment in his hand.

Suddenly from the north, there came a squall of such intensity that it sheared through the men's furs like a saber. A whirling, blue-white patch of snow appeared on the far edge of the deadwood. The men watched as it capered across the taiga like a two-legged sprite.

Kulik froze as the snow patch formed arms and hands and feet and danced through the taiga with a flurrying, magical gait, causing the Evenki's horses to rear and scream.

Run! Okhchen cried, as the Evenki shouted and spurred their trembling beasts. It is the demon of thunder! Run now!

I hear the sound of a door opening. Shrinking back from my screen, where the Evenki's thunder god is still gamboling, I gape at the beginnings of this story. What in the world? I don't understand how these words came out of my hands. Except for my *Astronomical Journal* articles, I've never written so much as a diary entry. This crazy narrative just sort of came over me, like a fever. I wrote it weirdly and quickly and effortlessly, less composing it than dreaming it.

I look up as a masked woman with long hair enters the chapel. She doesn't meet my eyes as she walks to the front row of benches and takes a seat. She bends her head. A hush descends again on the room. I rest my hands on my keyboard and don't type. My screen throws its halo toward her, marring the space's tranquility. The woman presses her hands to her face. She whispers to herself.

I click my computer shut and stuff it in my briefcase while listening to the woman's words. "Hail Mary, full of grace, the Lord is with thee. Blessed art thou among women, and blessed is the fruit of thy womb, Jesus. Holy Mary, mother of God, pray for us sinners now, and at the hour of death." Remaining motionless in the shadows, I can still feel the ragged edges of my report, with Okhchen yelling about demons and Kulik beginning to panic.

"Hail Mary full of grace," the woman softly says.

Kulik and the thunder god vanish as the woman's prayer raises a years-old memory of Paul's face, wan and tormented as he recovered from his first surgery. I get up and leave the chapel. The hallway outside is as lustrous as an optometrist's flashlight. I make my way to the hospital's exit, with its electric sliding doors, and go outside. Here there's a valet parking cars and a kiosk with coffee and pastries. I buy a coffee with milk and a bear claw wrapped in waxed paper. I find a metal bistro table and chair close to the kiosk and sit down. I lower my mask beneath my chin and inhale and exhale several times, willing myself to be calm. I drink my coffee and eat half my bear claw. After I've taken three bites, I realize that I should've washed or at least disinfected my hands before touching my food. Or maybe you shouldn't eat with your bare hands when they're covered with disinfectant? Did I read something about benzene? I wipe my fingers on the paper and get up and find a trash can and throw away the coffee cup and the other bear claw half. I approach the entrance and the doors slide open. A guard greets me with a stare. He sits at a table hosting an array of sanitizers. I rub the gel on my hands up to my wrists. It smells like fresh false lemon.

I pass by the waiting area. The seats in this space are brown, padded, and comfortable, but I don't want to be here. Sixteen years ago, I occupied this chair, the third one from the left, and my mother sat next to me. Actually, they were different chairs, or differently upholstered, but it doesn't matter because it was in this spot that my mother and I clenched through Paul's first radical resection. Mom helped me cope by telling me about a flying turtle who mistakenly thought it was a mighty eagle, a delusion that persisted until the day a French chef saw him sailing through the air and shot him with a rifle and turned him into a stew. I had been suggesting to her that, while her colorful fables about life's inevitable losses were poignant and instructive, maybe that day she could tell me a happier story. She could, for example, tell me about how the bullet missed and the turtle flew to the moon and the moon men were so amazed by its green skin and fancy shell that they welcomed the turtle into their lunar tribe, and everybody stayed excellent friends forever. My mother had responded with the sentiment that optimism is a form of hope and hope is painful and dangerous. Also, she wanted to know, why wasn't I crying? It was strange that I never cried, it's natural to cry, and if I had problems crying, I could cry about the turtle who was dumb enough to think it was an eagle, and maybe I would feel better. It was at this point that Paul's oncologist, Dr. Skinner, had walked up to us in her blue scrubs. Dr. Skinner looked at me very seriously and said, "Laura, hello, it's good to see you. How are you?"

I'd said, "Please tell me about Paul."

Dr. Skinner replied, "Paul was calling for someone named Jabulani."

"That's his father," I said.

"I see. Is he here?"

"No."

"Paul is not looking good, Laura."

"Will he live?" I asked, while my mother pressed her cheek onto mine and wept.

"We don't know," Dr. Skinner said. "We can't say yet."

"Can you give me his chances?" I asked.

"Generally, people actually don't find percentages that helpful, psychologically speaking."

"Please just tell me."

"Twenty percent," Dr. Skinner said. "Fifteen percent."

"But you said it was forty percent before," I'd said.

So now I pass by the brown padded chairs and make a loop past the Blood Diseases center and the Breast Health center and Urology. Masked attendants sit behind reception desks, and more doctors wearing bulky PPE gear walk quickly in and out of swinging doors. Patients and their family members, spaced six feet apart, stare at their phones while I skirt Neck and Head, Lung, and Gynecology. I find a spot by the far side of Colorectal, next to a synthetic fern, the same place where last year Dr. Skinner loped up to Mom and me after an endoscopy and said, "Everything looks great." I sit in the exact same chair as I did then and place my briefcase on the chair where my mother had sat next to me. I open the briefcase and extract my computer. I place the briefcase on my lap and the computer on the briefcase. I open the computer. I read what I've written and think that my stress must really be getting to me because I have no idea how I'm going to edit this into a recognizable congressional report.

Run! Okhchen cried, as the Evenki shouted and spurred their trembling beasts. Run now! Run away!

Still among the trees, Kulik and Krinov looked over their shoulders to see the Evenki galloping away from them across the tundra. The four fawn-brown stallions that drew their sledge slammed into one another as they chased after their masters. Kulik and Krinov leapt over the dead pines and larches, running madly toward their escaping vehicle as it careened over the thin sheets of snow. Krinov, with his long gait, leapt into the sledge with two bounds, while Kulik scampered forward haltingly on his little feet.

Jump! Krinov brayed, cackling beneath his fur hat, which had slid down over half his face. Jump, you insect without balls! Jump, you earwig without a cock!

Krinov reached out his long arm as Kulik hopped into the air, gripped onto his countryman's burly hand, and pulled himself aboard.

As they fell backwards in the sledge, the two men gazed in amazement at the blue-white wind twirling in the deadwood, the zephyr still flinging that bewitched smidge of snow so that it appeared a malefic elf with jittering arms and dancing hooves.

I assume you believe, with your heathen friends, that this little flurry is a demon endowed with the full gifts of the Archfiend himself? Krinov inquired.

They are a simple people, Kulik panted as the sledge battered over rocks and the Evenki shrilled their song into the air. There are always such risks of overreaction when one does fieldwork amongst native hordes who are bewildered by their own ignorance and terrors of the unknown.

That is precisely what I told your betters at the Academy, Krinov raged, when they begged me to oversee your little romp here amongst the wildlings. But poor Kulik is bewildered by his ignorance, I said. He is beset by the terrors of the unknown! His brain has been turned into pure fat on account of seeing a few souls fly to heaven from the banks of the Yalu!

Leave me alone, Kulik grumbled, as he steadied himself in his seat. He removed one of the pebbles from his pocket and attempted to examine the object with his bare eye, as he had lost his loupe in the harum-scarum caused by the snow sprite. Upon inspection, the little stone revealed itself to be an ordinary piece of black basalt, quite common to the area. If only he had stayed longer to search for evidence of an alien mineral, or even to find the crater!

Enough of this madness, Krinov thundered, slapping the rock out of Kulik's hand. Krinov threw his elbow around Kulik's scrawny neck and crushed him tightly to his chest, while Kulik clawed at his paws. No meteorite ever landed in the taiga, my son, Krinov breathed onto Kulik's whitening spectacles. You have been bedeviled by your tribulations, which have so scrambled your egg that you imagine cataclysms where none exist. Poor old Kulik, let your friend Krinov tell you your own story. You see, even before I met you, I had heard much about your idée fixe, and now that I have endured your flibbertigibbeting out here in the wastelands, I can see that your brief taste of combat has separated you from common sense as easily as a hussy is separated from her maidenhead.

Once there was a poor little mineralogist named Leonid Kulik, Krinov went on, as the sledge blasted through the snow. And this Kulik saw disasters wherever he looked. Why had he gone off his chump? Because in 1904, the Tsar sent our hero to war with the yapontsy in the far, far East. Now this was a just war, a fair war, a war that would warm any proper Russian's blood, as the Tsar was a good son of Ivan the Terrible and vowed to extend the sweet teats of the motherland all the way from the Black Sea to the outermost shores of Nippon. Yes, the Tsar ordered poor, stupid Kulik to abandon his beloved Academy studies of gneisses and schists and sail with his brethren from Leningrad to the Yalu River, a tributary that flowed like silk between Peking and Seoul. Kulik's battalion went to secure Port Arthur in Liaodong, but the yapontsy had different ideas and vowed to take the harbor from us with their samurai swords and their manly karate, threats our Army found quite risible until we discovered that they were metaphors and the enemy intended to use their howitzers against us instead. Poor old bumbling Kulik thus found himself quite surprised on that April morning, when he stood with his fellow dragoons on the banks of the Yalu and saw the puffs of smoke floating up from the yaponskiye cannons. As the shells came sailing down from the heavens, they caused tremors that sent Kulik flying up into the sky like a pigeon. Yes, the force sent him hurling over his screaming, bleeding brothers, and he felt for the first time a fear so exquisite that it addled his mind.

It addled his mind forever, Krinov said, his elbow still squeezing Kulik's neck while Kulik let his hands fall to his lap and stared at his countryman with wide, blazing eyes. Even after poor, little, stupid Kulik escaped the front, miraculously unharmed, and sailed back to Mother Russia, he could not but feel the *boom, boom, boom* of the mortars still rattling his bones. He felt his skeleton shake when he looked in the beautiful faces of the maidens strolling down Nevsky Prospekt, when he ate his porridge with his fat and doting mamushka in the morning, and when he stared down at his little rocks through his microscope, which he did for the next twenty-three years. For he could not free himself from his shock. He now believed that one must always be afraid of yapontsy, howitzers, and even the sky itself, because there is no safe place in the whole world.

This is why, years later, when he heard the rumors bruited by a few cranks and barbarians that the most unlikely thing had occurred on the earth—that a meteorite had fallen from the Siberian sky like Lucifer—he believed the tale. Our poor, stupid, idiotic, monkey-brained Kulik had been driven so mad by panic that he grew convinced, based on no proof, on the most ephemeral evidence, that great flaming balls of moon rock tumbled from the heavens with the regularity of raindrops, and are as ordinary as the commonplace idiocy of man.

While the sledge thrashed forward, and the Evenki raced toward Voranova, Kulik collapsed like a dead fish in the arms of Krinov, every part of him limp and helpless except for those eyes shining with hate. He had felt this emotion before, a loathing so agile it thrilled through his veins like fire. While crawling on the banks of the bloody Yalu River, he had directed this ire at the yapontsy and called upon the Most Holy Lady Theotokos for strength. But now, while Krinov throttled him, Kulik remembered the small brown face of Okhchen and the blue sprite that danced in the deadwood.

Kulik plunged a hand into his pocket and grasped his stones. Just as Okhchen had been schooled to fear demons by the voiskos and his shaman, *he* had learned bone-deep lessons when the howitzer's concussions sent him soaring over the Yalu's cadaver-ridden shores. From those harsh studies, he knew that only the shock from an enormous projectile could have felled the Siberian wood.

Fear is a great teacher, is all he said.

"Laura?"

I look up. Connie stands in front of me. Her black glasses glint from beneath her blue cap. She holds out a pair of blue gloves.

"Is it time yet?" I stand too quickly, so that my computer falls to the floor with a bang.

"Oh, watch it there, hon."

"Is it over? Is he all right?" I snatch up the computer and shut it and jam it into my briefcase. "Is there a problem?"

"No, everything's fine. We just got him in early because there was a cancellation."

"Is he awake?"

She gives me the gloves, which have the thin, squeaky consistency of rubber balloons. "Coming to, now in post-op. Let's go see him."

"Did you find anything?"

"Oh, we have to ask the doctor," she says, her eyes smiling behind her lenses.

I snap on the gloves and pick up my briefcase. Connie turns around and leads me to the elevators. We pass new and different patients and family members who hunch in the brown chairs in the waiting area. They stare at their phones and seem identical to the other people who arrived here early, at the same time that Paul and I did. Or maybe they are the same people. I look at a wall clock and see that it's 11:30 AM. My limbs feel loose, and I'm shaking again, suddenly.

My mind oscillates like a dragonfly's wing, moving back and forth between the cliff edge of this moment and the soothing order of the writing. History doesn't tell us what happened to the Evenki leader Vasily Okhchen, who, after being persuaded to lead the Soviets into the ruined forest, would provide Kulik with an extensive first-person account of the blue fire that filled the sky on the morning of June 30, 1908. Yevgeny Krinov, Kulik's unhelpful colleague, later burned the hundreds of nitrate film negatives of Kulik's unique photographs of the Siberian deadwood, for reasons that some attribute to ignorance and others to spite. As for Leonid Kulik himself, he held fast to his theory that a meteorite caused the 1908 Tunguska disaster, even though he couldn't prove it. Today, almost all astronomers agree with Kulik that a minor planet caused the Tunguska event, though professional consensus holds that the meteor vaporized completely, a common enough phenomenon in the history of hazardous objects and possibly the reason why Kulik never found the evidence he sought.

My thoughts of Kulik and Okhchen and Krinov disintegrate

as I follow Connie beyond Blood Draw and toward the elevators. We walk by a large window that shows the orange sun cloaked with a veil of wildfire smoke so invasive it resembles a monster. I listen to the squeak and rustle of Connie's shoes, which are enveloped in blue booties. I wonder if I also should put on booties. In Wuhan's Huoshenshan Hospital, the swabs of the computer mice and floors showed that SARS-COV-2 floated in the air like atomized meteor fragments before they landed all over the place. That means that here, in the hospital, as I perspire behind my mask and feel the strange rubber otherness of my gloved hand gripping onto my briefcase handle, I'm walking through a blast wave of virus. We all are. But my husband is in post-op, and he can't get sick for any reason, including my somehow giving him COVID from my shoes. My husband Paul is a Black man. Studies show not only that COVID flies through Wuhan and American hospitals like smoke or the demons of the eastern taiga. They reveal also that hospital algorithms are more likely to assign Black men, Black people like Paul and my son, lower risk scores than equally ill white people, lower risk scores even though they face a greater statistical probability than white people of suffering diseases like diabetes and kidney failure. Also, they're more apt to die from SARS-COV-2 than other racial groups because of I do not know why. Research on the question of COVID's racism is ongoing but the reasons are probably the same old reasons that we always hear and that relate also to the reasons why I don't want Tomás to go to those protests without my protection, which is because the police might kill him.

"Put on your booties, hon," Connie says. We're on the fifth floor. It's busier here. A network of hallways leads to a unit filled with little curtained rooms where patients recover from biopsies, surgeries, and tests that require general anesthesia. Nurses and nurses' attendants and doctors move purposefully from bed to bed. By the entrance, where I'm still standing, I see a large box filled with a blue cloud of slippers. Next to the box stand several half-empty bottles of citrus hand sanitizer. I put down my briefcase and lean against the wall and slip booties over my shoes. When I look back up, Connie's already walking into a bay. Paul lies in a bed, while Dr. Skinner, blond and six feet tall, stands above him like a benevolent stork. She talks from behind a clear plastic face shield and a mask. A brown plastic chair sits by the bed. Paul's face is naked. A large computer with a graph-filled monitor stands by the far left wall, beeping rhythmically.

"Hey, Laura," Dr. Skinner says.

"Hi." I put down my briefcase and go over to Paul. My husband's eyes glow with propofol and love; his cheeks look somehow flattened. I've seen this before, post-surgery. By tomorrow or the next day, he'll be normal again. I kiss Paul's cool forehead and then his lips through my mask.

"Everything's good," he says, his hand fumbling on my face, so my mask goes askew.

"Yes, it looked good," Dr. Skinner says.

"Okay," I say.

"How long were you waiting?" he asks.

"Not long, babe," I answer, as Paul closes his eyes and seems to fall asleep. I turn to Dr. Skinner. "What did you see?"

"She didn't see anything," Paul says, with his eyes still closed.

"Everything looked fine." The plastic shield, reflecting the room's fluorescents, sits like a flashing spaceship over Dr. Skinner's face. I can't see her expression.

I finally absorb the information, and a small explosion of light ignites in my chest. "That's good."

"We might have seen a few little changes, but we think it's the trauma from past surgeries and biopsies," she says then.

The explosion of light shrinks and dies. "What does that mean?"

"That we can go home," Paul says.

"That's right, that you can go home," Dr. Skinner says.

"But could the changes be bad?"

"We don't think so," she says. "We'll do a pathology and look at the blood panel, and if everything's fine, we'll check again in two or three months."

"See?" Paul squeezes my hand. His eyes are still closed. "Did you wait for long?"

"No babe," I say. "So, doctor, you're saying the changes aren't bad."

"We'll check back in two or three months, and I think it all looks good," Dr. Skinner says.

"Yeah, he did real good," Connie says, from the door.

"I always do good." Paul smiles. "Those drugs are good."

The two women laugh.

Dr. Skinner moves toward me and half reaches out her gloved hand, as if to touch my shoulder, which she often does after her consultations. She stops abruptly and puts her hand back down.

"Okay?" she asks. "Because it's okay."

"Okay," I say.

"Okay," Dr. Skinner says.

"Okay," Paul says.

"I'll swing back in maybe twenty minutes to see if he's good to go," Connie says.

Dr. Skinner and Connie leave. I sit in the chair and look at Paul, who mumbles something. The room is cold, and I have to pee. I press Paul's hand to my muzzled mouth. I want to put his fingers under my mask and kiss them with my bare lips, but I can't think in a normal way and don't know if I should sanitize my face before I do this.

"Were you waiting long?" he whispers.

"No, baby," I say.

Later that night, after we've come home, and Tomás and I help a drowsy Paul get into bed, there's a new problem. I'm in the kitchen, swiftly organizing my printouts on Tunguska and grabbing the green notebook so I can pack them. My mother lounges in the TV room. Tomás is in his bedroom talking with Cecil on the phone in a high, angry voice, probably about the protest that he didn't attend this afternoon. The air conditioner in the hallway chatters like an agitated woman. It's broken two times from overuse in the past six years, and I have to get it fixed again, and replace the air filter so we don't inhale the particulates from outside, and then also get the leaking pipe under the sink repaired. But I can't think of that now.

Three minutes ago, my phone began beeping while I read what seemed like one continuous news story. Today the former head of the CDC said he believes that the White House's response to COVID is a "failure," Donald Trump held a rally in Fayetteville, North Carolina, where he talked about how he loves budgets but first has to rebuild the military because it's been totally depleted, and Rochester police chief La'Ron Singletary resigned over the death of Daniel Prude—and then my screen flashed. A black band appeared across the iPhone's shiny surface notifying me of an EVACUATION ALERT for Pasadena. The Bobcat Fire at this moment rushes toward our home, spurred on by rapid winds and something called heavy fuels. No evacuation orders have been issued, but the warning says we should "Get Set" by assembling "supplies" and preparing to flee at any time.

I move away from the table and knock my notebook onto the floor, where it opens to sketches I've made of potential satellite trajectories. I leave it. I walk from the kitchen to the TV room. My mother sits in her chintz chair with her eyes closed. The television soundlessly exhibits images of females shouting while their glossy hair erupts from their heads like volcanoes.

"Mom," I say.

"Mmm."

"We have to get our stuff together, just in case."

"What?"

"The fire situation is looking not so great."

"This smoke junk in the air all the time is wacala."

"We have to get ready."

"Yeah," she says. "That's fine, I don't need anything."

"Mom."

"All I need is you and Paul and the kid."

"Come on, I'm exhausted."

She opens her eyes and nods when she sees my face. "Do we gotta go right now?"

"No. We just have to wait and see."

She closes her eyes again. "Ah, they're always saying crap like that. It's the end of the world, it's the end of the world. They don't know from the end of the world. I, on the other hand, know from the end of the world. Though I never told you about any of it because I don't want you to know what I went through."

I walk out of the living room and down the hall and tiptoe into our bedroom. I begin laughing silently so that tears stream down my cheeks. I ignore this. The room is dark and warm. I can see Paul's head on his pillow and the long shape of him beneath the sheet. His shoulder rises and falls, as he sleeps the deep sleep induced by the residue of the anesthesia. I wipe my face and go to our closet, which sits behind mirrored sliding doors. I open the doors and rummage through our clothes until I touch two duffels I've stored on the floor. I take the bags out and move to the bureau that stands against the far west wall. My head feels as poppable as a balloon animal. I open the drawers and scoop out underwear, T-shirts, and sweatpants. I go back to the closet and get Paul's jeans. I don't know what to take. My green plaid nightgown, his briefs. I return to the bureau and get three pairs of white tube socks of indeterminate sizes. I should have done this before, when I first began to realize that Southern California was turning into a seasonal inferno. I'm an idiot.

Paul shifts in the bed. "Laura?"

"You're okay," I say.

I approach Paul, but when I bend down to kiss him, I feel the soft pulse of his slumbering breath. I adjust his blanket, grab the duffels, and move out of the bedroom. I close the door with my foot and elbow and stand in the hallway. I hurry past my mother's wall of watercolors and enter Paul's office. A laptop sits on his desk, along with several framed photographs. Besides our wedding picture and an image of Tomás as a baby, one shot in a silver frame shows Paul's mother and father standing together, slim and serious in the preppy madras styles of 1960s Frankfort. Another picture shows just his father, Jabulani. Jabulani had a round, young face and kind eyes. His mouth resembles Paul's, but he doesn't smile. I remember how Dr. Skinner had said that Paul called out for his father at some point during his first surgery, a decade and a half ago. I unplug the computer from the wall and slip it into Paul's bag. I take the photo of his parents and the one of his father and put those in too.

"Laura," my mother says. Her voice comes from the kitchen. "Laurita."

"Ye-es." I put the duffels down and struggle to zip them. I half manage this and carry them clankingly out of the office and into the foyer. As I place the bags by the front door, my mother pads out, holding the notebook I'd knocked onto the kitchen floor.

"What are these?" she asks.

"Did you pack?" I ask.

"Your sketches look like flowers, like I used to do."

"You have to get your medicines and just a couple dresses, some extra sneakers."

"Hmm?" She stares at my notebook. "You're making roses like me."

I shake my head. "What?"

She opens the notebook and smiles widely as she shows me one my loopy models.

"That's a projected flight plan of an earth-returning satellite programmed to detect NEOS."

She puts her arms around me. "You used to like to draw, you remember? When you were little, you made so many pretty pictures. You got that from me, you know."

"Your medications and toothbrush and socks." My voice muffles as she presses my face into her neck. "A nightgown. Maybe a book or some magazines. Underwear."

"Are you crying?"

For a few seconds, I let my face rest in the cool cradle of my mother's neck. I'd like to lie down in her lap like I did when we were in the hospital chapel so long ago. But as soon as I feel her take my weight, I have a brief sensation of giving way. *Steady,* I tell myself. *Steady, lady.* I kiss her on the cheek and release myself. I crouch down and check Paul's bag to make sure I packed his briefs. "I don't know."

"Okay, honey." She opens the notebook again and looks at it.

I make my way through the foyer and dining area to Tomás's room. I follow my son's complex music, which sounds like men gently arguing. His door is open about three inches, and I can see that he's shirtless and lying down on his stomach on his bed while looking at his phone.

"I love you, I love you so much," my son is saying, in a voice I've never heard before.

"I love you too," I hear Cecil reply.

Tomás flips over onto his back, takes up his phone, and hovers it above his body—over his chest, ribs and on downward while wriggling on the bed. "All of this is for you, it will always be only for you," he says. "Do you like my skin?"

"Yes."

"Do you like my stomach?"

"Yes."

"Do you like my—"

I move away swiftly from the door and stand in the hallway. I run my hands over my face and stare down at the carpet. I support everything that is happening here except that the Bobcat Fire is burning in heavy fuels, and I don't want to see my son being sexy. Or hear him being sexy. Or read about him being sexy. Cecil Bautista is tall, muscular, and possesses a set of long shining limbs that spent most of last year twined around my son. Cecil failed out of advanced calculus. However, he writes a great deal of verse, verse without capital letters, verse that so passionately declares his lust and love for Tomás that last year Dr. Williams—Cecil and Tomás's English III Honors teacher—called Cecil's mother, Blessica, Paul, and me into a meeting. Once we all found ourselves arrayed in front of her desk like detained adolescents, she requested that we review Cecil's spondees and expressed her concern that our children's relationship had become "obsessive." Paul smiled at the poems while observing diplomatically that we were capable of supervising our son's emotional well-being. I blinked at Cecil's astonishing use of transitive verbs and managed to accuse Dr. Williams of homophobia. "And you evidently also do not understand contemporary poetry, Madam," Blessica added. After that we had no more trouble. Though of course they are deeply, deeply obsessive.

"Mom?" I hear.

"Hey." I move back to the doorway. Tomás struggles to put on his shirt while still holding onto his phone and laughing at something I don't understand.

"Hey, Mrs. Mthembu," I hear Cecil say, using my husband's

name, like everyone else at his school does, even though I still use my own name. But I don't care about things like that anymore.

"Hey, Cecil. Um, so, Tomás, it looks like we have to pack a bag."

"What?" Tomás looks at his phone and widens his eyes.

"Everything's okay." Beneath my button-down shirt, sweat drips between my breasts. "Just in case. The fire's getting a little—"

"Do we have to evacuate?" I hear Cecil ask.

"Not necessarily. We're just being told to get ready." I try to remember what I read on my phone. "I think they are evacuating Sierra Madre."

"I better go tell my mom," Cecil says.

"He's not in danger, they're in Studio City," I tell my son.

"Are you going to be okay?" Tomás breathes.

The boys interrogate each other's relative safety in an elongated and difficult-to-follow conference while I continue standing in the doorway and attempt to explain that a tsunami of wildfire may very well be heading in our personal direction and maybe, if my son would like us to survive, he could pack his jeans, underwear, computer, and retainer.

"Your orange bag," I'm saying, just as my mother wanders by, still scrutinizing my notebook. She has a pen in her hand.

"Can you help me?" I ask her.

Mom looks at me and then looks at Tomás. "Hey, kid, pack your crap in your bag."

"I love you so, so, so, much," Tomás whispers into his phone.

"Get off that goddam thing, mister," my mother is yelling, "before we all burn up like the Hindenburg."

Shaking, I walk down the hall and go to Paul's and my bedroom. When I open the door, though, I realize I don't know where my phone is. I go to Paul's office, where it's not. Then I go to the kitchen and find it on the table, next to my printouts. I pick it up and put it in my pants pocket. I worry that I should pack water and food and put it in the car in the event that we have to flee for our lives and this somehow precludes our access to grocery stores. I spend the next half hour listening to my mother order Tomás around while I throw apples, bagels, cheese, and cold packs into a cooler and place it in the back of the Volvo. I also find a carton of bottled water and put that next to the cooler before shutting the trunk. Back in the house, Tomás is now silent, and my mother has turned on the sound of the television. I don't know if either of them has packed. I return to our bedroom and close the door behind me.

I lie next to Paul, who doesn't stir when my body presses into the mattress. I curl my legs around him and click on my phone, scrolling through the warnings. Paul breathes, a heavy beat. While keeping my eyes on a page called "Pasadena Now," I try to follow his slow respirational pace with my own breath. I inhale long, steady skeins of air. I exhale. I feel the heat coming off my husband's neck. I extend my legs and touch the roughness of his bare feet with my toes. I hear the bang of a firecracker, far off. I'll have to stay awake tonight, I tell myself, in case we have to run. The cinders travel for miles and ignite dry autumn grass. But a person has to retain her presence of mind. A parent must retain her composure—it occurs to me suddenly that I didn't even check on Tomás's homework today. Or yesterday. I don't know if he is keeping up with his studies. I've failed. The studies of studying say that lax COVID homeschooling leads to increased ignorance and a galactic drop in intelligence that will be felt for generations.

I breathe, breathe, and breathe, lightly clasping Paul around his ribs. In the science of asteroid orbit projection, we engage in nonlinear analyses. Because it's so difficult to estimate the trajectory that a Near-Earth Object will follow in, say, fifty years, we find ourselves caught in the grip of "uncertainty growth" and have to imagine a wide assortment of possible futures. We construct models of virtual asteroids and see what disasters they might cause. While this analytic methodology helps us guard against a potentially deadly meteorite impact, it's an unhelpful personal practice if one seeks to maintain one's social and psychological "grip." Caught in the vortex of my own personal uncertainty growth, I can fathom a thousand, million different ways to lose the people I love, but if I panic, this family could fall apart.

People have endured worse before, I remind myself. I push my thumb on my phone screen, revealing pictures of nearby Mount Wilson, which blooms with roses of fire. I let my phone drop and press my cheek against Paul's thin back, kissing his spine while he sleeps. After all, think about everything the Evenki went through. One morning they looked up and saw the sky open up like a mouth, I tell myself as I close my eyes and will my breath to come at a slower pace. Blue fire filled the heavens, and they were blinded. The flames came down, and then the storms. *Crack, crack, crack, crack, crack.* A wind knocked the people to the ground and the fire blistered their skins, I dream. Then the trees fell, like soldiers on the banks of the Yalu River, like the Evenki under the guns of the voiskos. Okhchen's dealings with the Soviets had taught him that important lessons lay in terrible things. While his body boiled and the world split in half, he analyzed the data and read the signs, in order to protect his people. And much later, in the middle of the deadwood, this savvy man saw a small spirit whirling, warning him with its snow-flinging dance. "Do not enter," it said to Okhchen. "Do not enter. Do not enter," said the terrible god of thunder.

3
I'm the Only Person Who's Ever Been Touched by a Star

"I do not see what the problem is," Paul says.

"Your theory is unfalsifiable," answers a male voice on his computer.

"We've talked about this before, basalt is too common to be a reliable indicator," says another male voice. "It's like saying dirt proves a prior impact."

"I am not saying any such thing," Paul responds, tapping a pencil on his desk. He's in the midst of the annual Asteroids, Comets, and Meteors conference, which this year takes place virtually. He sits in his ergonomic chair in a white shirt, gray sweatpants, and bare feet. He stares into the monitor. The computer's speaker broadcasts the aggressive yawps of scientists commenting on his most recent, unpublished paper.

"Maybe the presence of basalt shows that there was a meteorite, or maybe it was caused by plate shifting, or a volcano, or maybe it's just part of the upper crust," says a third male voice. "There's no way to tell."

"Paul, you are very well respected for your work on

left-handed acids found in—in—" says one of the voices, I don't know which one.

"Tagish Lake meteorites," says another voice.

"Thank you," Paul says stiffly.

"But I don't see this theory as being helpful or even that interesting," the other, previous voice continues. "You're suggesting that we've been hit millions or even billions of times—"

"That something is frightening does not make it untrue," Paul says.

I am hovering in the hallway, eavesdropping. Six days have elapsed since the evacuation warning, which remains in place, but the sun no longer looks that crazy orange color. On my phone, it says that the high today in Pasadena will reach 90 degrees. The air quality index now reads yellow, for Moderate, as opposed to purple, which means Very Unhealthy and lasted for more than a week. We can go outside again and breathe with less fear, even though the horizon still looks like a dirty mattress. During the worst of it, I hadn't been able to get my hands on N95 masks, so whenever I left the house to take out the garbage, I wrapped two of Paul's T-shirts around my face.

Through this period, Tomás sulked like a vampire in his room, my mother spent hundreds of dollars on shopping sites and streamed reality television, and my husband stayed in his office, administering final touches to the paper now succumbing to scholarly vivisection. I see Paul clutch his pencil as if he were strangling a mouse, so I close the office door and make my way to Mom's bedroom. I poke my head into the space that used to be my study and where, before March of 2020, I spent most evenings and weekends writing treatises at my walnut desk. She's not here, though; the room stands empty.

I go to the kitchen. Tomás wears a surgical mask and bends over the stove in sweaty deliberation. Thick white steam rises from four different pots. With one hand, he grips a wooden spoon that he uses to stir a Dutch oven filled with pork rind and beans. In the other, he holds Julia Child's *Mastering the Art of French Cooking*. He squints at the cookbook as if it contains the as-yet-unsolved set of vector analysis problems that I assigned him more than a week ago.

"Don't breathe on any of the food," Tomás says, as I kiss him on the cheek.

"Aren't you taking this a little far?"

"His mom is really scared."

"Okay, but isn't lunch tomorrow?"

"It takes at least two days to make a proper cassoulet."

"Cassoulet is just a fancy word for chili, and chili's easy, you just slap it together."

"Then it wouldn't be special."

I shake my head. "Where's Grandma?"

He opens the refrigerator and extracts some herbs. "Napping, I think."

I leave the kitchen and move toward the TV room. Instead of presiding in her customary chair, my mother sits on throw pillows strewn on the beige wall-to-wall carpet and props her back against our leather sofa. Next to her left foot, my green notebook is open wide to the pages where I'd sketched satellite trajectories. Three nearly untouched watercolor sets are propped up in front of her. My Caltech coffee mug overflows with paint-tainted water. She bends over and paints on a large white pad of paper, while the television silently plays another iteration of the show about the women with the volcano hair and the shrieking.

"Are they upset because of COVID?" I ask.

"No, the skinny redhead is an alcoholic and is mad because the others don't care." She makes big, black loops with her brush. "Come here, I'm going to show you something."

I move closer and stare down at the little drawings of ellipses scrawled in my notebook. I also examine my mother's large and dramatic, curlicue-infused, flowerlike shapes.

"Where'd you get this stuff?"

"Amazon." Mom dips her paintbrush into my coffee mug and then jams it into a black cake in one of the watercolor sets. She swirls the paintbrush on the paper, sending dark droplets flying onto the carpet. "Your problem is your line."

"My line."

"Your line on your flowers."

"Those aren't flowers. They're possible routes for satellites that could search for NEOS and then return to Earth. We don't have an asteroid detection system in place, and we really probably need one. If we sent out satellites in this configuration, we might be able to—"

My mother bats her hand at me. "You didn't notice the similarity?"

"What?"

"You could do it better, which is what I'm trying to teach you."

"Mom, I'm a radar astronomer."

"You were always good at drawing when you were a baby. But your problem is your line, you need a strong line," she says. "Look how I do it."

"Okay."

"You see how wonderful this is," she says, turning another page on her pad and daubing it with huge, black gyres that look nothing like my satellite orbits, because if NASA programmed a satellite with this flight plan, it would crash back into the earth in a fireball-spewing explosion costing the federal government hundreds of millions of dollars.

"What's this one called?" I ask.

"*George Vincent Brooks's Rose,*" she says softly.

I touch her shoulder.

She continues painting as a tear falls down her cheek.

"Why don't you use the colors?" I ask finally.

"Oh, no, I can't do that yet." She pats the tears away delicately, so as to preserve the scrollwork around her eyes. "Like I'm telling you, a painter must first work on her line. I never got past that stage before you-know-who. I have to perfect my line before I can graduate to using pigments."

"Oh, right."

We both look down at her drawing. It bears about as much similarity to a rose as it does to a satellite orbit, but, as I study the shape, I see that it does resemble the spiraling I've been doing lately.

I'm quiet for a few minutes, watching her paint.

"Well, it's good, Mom," I finally say.

She laughs up at me, grabbing my calf and giving it a good squeeze.

It's time to clean again. I can't do the kitchen since Tomás remains in there, cutting up lamb for the socially distanced luncheon that we're going to host tomorrow. Yesterday, Paul swabbed the foyer with Pine Sol and swept the dining room floor, so I don't have to deal with that. However, the day before, Mom "took care" of the second bathroom, and her housekeeping methodology consists of reading *the National Enquirer* on my iPad while sitting on the bathtub's edge and blowing clandestine cigarette smoke out of the little transom window. So I'll start there.

I bring in the bucket and bottles. I pour out the clear yellow soap. I run the sponge under the bathtub's faucet. The liquid cleanser looks like thick chardonnay I'd like to drink; when mingled with water it expands into a silky cloud. I get on my knees and press the lather onto the bathtub floor. I make a string of foaming parabolas, rinse, and scrub again. My reflection in the porcelain is dark and hazy, moving in flashes and fragments. After that, I wipe down the translucent shower curtain. The sink. The toilet.

I spray Windex on a Brawny towel and press germless circles into the mirror while thinking of a paper published at the beginning of the pandemic. Yale and UCLA professors came out with an e-report concluding that 40 percent of U.S. COVID fatalities occurred in nursing homes, probably because of infections spread by staff who worked several jobs and commuted between different care facilities. Perhaps predictably, the *Los Angeles Times* recommended in April that adult children who care even a little bit about their parents should remove them from any and all senior living communities that now sounded like incubators of death. In an article that would eventually cost me both my home office and my illusions about my own judgment, a doctor was quoted saying reasonable things about the precautionary principle, but between the lines you could really hear him assessing that only a sociopath would right now be stowing their mother in group housing run by peripatetic strangers. Fifteen minutes after reading that data, I'd started preparations for rescuing Mom from her place at Golden Breezes. The next day, I dismantled my study to make way for her new bedroom while she happily shuffled around our house in soft socks, even though she'd broken her leg through similar shenanigans not two and a half years earlier.

I grab the plastic bottle of soap and squeeze more on my sponge. I scrub the porcelain again.

I rinse and repeat, not able to tell when the tub is clean enough. In a report I read last month, Dr. Bruce Aylward of the World Health Organization and Dr. Wannian Liang of the Beijing Health Bureau concluded that a majority of COVID clusters in the People's Republic of China have erupted among relatives. The researchers determined that, rather than exploding from the nursing care facilities from which we've been encouraged to remove our mothers, the largest share of infections in that country have spread through family contact in the home.

I push away from the bathtub and sit on the closed toilet. I look up at the transom window, the one my mother uses to blow out the smoke from her slim Capris, the same Capris she likes to operatically promise on her own life that she's not smoking. The sky remains low and brown; the Bobcat Fire continues to claw its way toward my family. I reach over to open the tap and flick on the overhead shower. The blast of water swirls all the suds away. Even with this racket, I can hear my mother singing in the TV room while she's probably buying more art supplies on Amazon. *La la la, lalalalala, la la la la,* she croons. It's the theme song from that Beverly Hills Housewives show. I feel the showerhead's droplets wetting my hair and realize, even if we made a mistake in bringing her home, I couldn't get her out of this house now if I used a crowbar and explosives.

"Cassoulet usually takes three or four days to prepare, so I had to do some shortcuts," Tomás is saying.

It's the next day, at noon. Cecil and his mother, Blessica, who is an E.R. surgeon, will arrive at our house at any minute. The temperature has dropped to the 80s, and the air quality meter on my phone still reads Moderate. Tomás's cassoulet bubbles in the oven. A large bowl of leafy green salad sits in the refrigerator, alongside a bottle of cooling Zinfandel for the adults and a six-pack of flavored mineral water for the boys. This morning, my son carted out six metal folding chairs from the garage and got Paul to help him hoist the kitchen table onto the lawn. Tomás put two chairs on the far side of the grass and four chairs on the other side. The table shines with a freshly ironed white linen tablecloth and stacks of squeaky-clean cups, plates, knives, forks, spoons, and linen napkins.

"It smells good," Mom says. We're all in the kitchen. Everybody has a mask slung around their chins except for her.

Paul opens up the refrigerator. "Let's eat."

"We have to wait until they get here," Tomás says, closing it again.

I flap a hand at the fridge. "I can't believe everything you've made."

"I should bring the cassoulet outside so it can cool," Tomás says. "Do we have a trivet?"

"It's in the second drawer on the left."

Tomás digs through a drawer. "Mom, did you taste the beans?"

"They're good."

"They're perfect," my mother says.

"Let me just have some now, because I can't wait," Paul says.

"No!" Tomás turns off the oven and slips on a pair of red oven mitts. He puts the trivet under his armpit and pulls out the pot. While his father opens the back door, he carries the food out to the backyard.

"Don't burn yourself," my mother calls after him.

I nudge Paul. "He cooked all of that."

"I know," Paul says.

"He's a good boy," Mom says.

"He's never cooked anything in his life," I say.

"He's cooked sandwiches," she answers.

"That's not cooking," I laugh.

Paul looks in the refrigerator again. "He's in love."

The doorbell rings. Tomás comes running back inside, his face already swaddled.

"Put on your masks, Blessica's really crazy about that stuff."

"Do I have to?" Mom touches her face. "I put on lipstick."

"Grandma."

"Masks make me look old." My mother presses her hands against her two-tone hair. "Also, I don't have to if I don't want. I have osteoporosis."

"Grandma!" Tomás runs toward the front door.

"Really?" I say.

Mom shrugs. "You know." She sails out of the kitchen and into the hall while Paul and I pull our masks up.

Tomás returns with Blessica and Cecil. Even with half his face covered, Cecil strides into the kitchen looking like a film star, as if Rob Lowe had a child with Denzel Washington, the only two cinematic references for great male beauty that I can call up easily, on account of my antiquity. Blessica follows him, petite, with shining, too-long hair and a tidy, red dress. She carries a large, stuffed, woven bag and hovers in the doorway, while the two boys stare at each other with beaming eyes.

The adults all say, "Hi!" and then Blessica blurts, "We should go outside."

"It's safer there," I say.

"Indoor aerosols," Blessica says.

"Chances of transmitting outdoors with safety protocols are almost zero," I say. "According to the latest study."

"Let's have a nice lunch," Paul says. "Tomás worked so hard."

"Come on." Blessica pushes Cecil out the back door and into the yard. Tomás follows, chattering at them.

Paul gets the wine bottle and the six-pack out of the refrigerator. I grab the corkscrew from a bottom drawer and a roll of paper towels from a cabinet.

"Mom!" I yell out.

"Nuh uh," she says, as she makes her way to the TV room.

Paul and I go outside. Blessica, Cecil, and Tomás stand around the table. Blessica's shaking her head.

"I thought Cecil told you that we're only comfortable eating our own food," Blessica's saying.

"We brought some tuna sandwiches," Cecil implores Tomás.

"But I was really careful," Tomás says. "I didn't breathe on any of it."

I try to smile, and it hurts my face. "There's nothing that says that you can get infected from another person's cooking."

"I'm sorry, but we're not taking any chances." Blessica shows me the inside of her bag. It bulges with Tupperware containers, forks and spoons, two bottles of water, and paper plates.

"My grandson cooked all that food for you," my mother yells from the open window of the TV room, which gives her easy screaming access to the yard.

"That's why you can eat takeout," I say. "It doesn't infect you."

"From seeing what I've seen at hospital, I trust nothing," Blessica says. "Colleagues getting sick, and two dying, despite taking every precaution." She touches Cecil on the elbow without seeming conscious of the gesture. "Also, the COVID tests, we assume that you took them."

We all look at her.

"Or maybe you *didn't* get tested," she says bitterly.

"Mom!" Cecil says.

"We've been really, really careful," I say, not mentioning that since she's an E.R. doctor, she's the one who's high risk and maybe we're the ones who should be worried. "And the tests aren't always accurate."

"Mom, come on."

"Everything's good, Bless," Paul says. "Laura has forced us all to be ridiculously cautious."

"Right," Blessica says, pressing her eyes with her thumb and ring finger. "I mean, I don't know."

"I'm sorry about the food," Cecil says to Tomás.

"It's all right," Tomás says, "I don't care."

"It smells good," Cecil says.

"Julia Child," Tomás says.

"I have to keep this child alive, just so you understand," Blessica says.

"Cassoulet takes three or four days to cook right," my mother yells out the window.

I look at Tomás. His eyes are red. I say, "Of course it's fine."

"It's fine," Tomás says.

"Okay," Blessica says, defeated. "If we're going to do this, let's just do it."

"Yeah, let's eat," Paul says.

Blessica and Cecil go over to the two chairs on the far side of the lawn. They sit down and take out their Tupperware containers and their other gear, which spills out onto their laps. Paul, Tomás, and I ladle cassoulet onto our porcelain plates. Neither Paul nor I feel like drinking alcohol, so all three of us grab mineral waters. We walk over to our chairs and sit down and try to balance everything on our knees.

"I should have gotten littler tables, sorry," Tomás says.

"It's great," Cecil says from far down the grass.

We all take off our masks and begin to eat.

"Honey, it's so good," I say.

"The beans are good," Paul says. "The chicken is good."

"It's lamb," Tomás says.

"Lamb!" Paul says.

Cecil unwraps a sandwich. "It smells so good."

"Very, very nice," Blessica says.

"You look nice," Tomás says, to Cecil.

"You look nice, too," Cecil says.

"Is that a new shirt?" Tomás asks.

"No, it's that one I got from Uniqlo last year."

"Oh, yeah."

The boys pick at their food, glaring at their plates. All the adults make encouraging eating noises.

"You guys should talk," Blessica says, after a while. "That's why we're here."

They both nod, still staring at their laps.

My maskless mother comes out. Her eyes are on Tomás. She smiles at him, but he's bent his head, and his lips are moving like he's talking to himself. She looks at Cecil. Cecil's a good kid and smiles back at her and then looks down, puckering his forehead. Mom goes over to the table and exclaims over the superlative quality of the food. She ladles a huge portion out for herself and asks Paul to open up the wine. He pours her a glass, and she settles into her chair, gingerly, and doesn't complain about how hard the metal seat feels on her hip. I offer to get her a pillow, and she says that she has a nice big behind, which is plenty of cushion. She drinks her wine and puts the glass on the grass. She lifts up her plate and inhales the cassoulet as if she's a mime attempting to communicate how wonderful it smells. She doesn't eat it. She puts her plate down on the grass and picks her glass back up. She drains it with a flourish. Paul pours her a refill. Meanwhile, the boys remain mute. Tomás shreds his lamb into tiny slivers. Cecil tightens his hands around his sandwich. Blessica and I look at each other. Blessica shrugs.

"So," my mother says.

"I can taste the pork," I say.

"So," my mother says again. "I heard a story once that I'm going to tell you just to pass the time as we all eat—or should be eating—Tomás's wonderful food."

Blessica frowns down at her sandwich but doesn't say anything.

"Once there was a girl, very young, very beautiful, very artistic, and very stupid," my mother goes on. "She met a man. He was tall. Handsome. Older. Rich. And he brought her a single red rose, making her believe that he loved her and that the rest of her life would be diamonds and cake. And so this girl, after getting beaten around the head by her mother, decided that yes, she loved this man and she'd marry him. The only problem was, when she lay her head on her new husband's chest at night, she couldn't hear his heartbeat. Also, one day, when he cut himself shaving, she saw that no blood ran down his face. She noticed that he could pick up a car with one hand and throw it over his shoulder when he wanted to steal somebody's parking spot, but when they walked by a church, he would faint. Finally, on their first anniversary, the girl woke up to find her husband twirling around the living room, with his mouth stained bright red. 'What is going on?' she asked. Her husband laughed like a maniac, ran to the bathroom, and dragged out the dead body of the village priest. 'I'm drunk, I'm drunk,' he sang, stooping down to bite the priest's neck. And so that's how the girl discovered that, instead of marrying a rich, older man who knew how to treat a girl right, she'd married a zombie."

Tomás wipes his eyes. "Grandma."

"For a while, the girl tried to make the zombie husband happy because even if he was a zombie, they were still married in the eyes of the church, and if she got a divorce the money would dry up and her mother would call her a whore. So she turned a blind eye whenever the zombie brought home one of his victims, and she drank wine whenever he ate the neighbors. One day, he dragged a half-dead fisherman into the living room and slowly nibbled him, finger by finger, toe by toe, the liver, the heart, and, as the finale, the delicious brains. The week after that it was an infant child, and later it was the postman, and then it was a farmer who cut down sugar cane with a big machete. Every time the zombie finished with the corpses, he and the girl would twirl around the room, singing, 'I'm drunk, I'm drunk.' And so it went until the day he gave the girl a nasty, hungry look, and she knew he wanted to make her his next meal.

"So what she did was, she said, 'I think we should get a divorce.' This is when the zombie husband's eyes shot out lasers and his fangs grew pointy. He flew up to the ceiling, shouting at her that she was a bad wife who couldn't draw worth a damn, and while he was bitching at her, she ran to the backyard where he had put the machete after eating the sugarcane farmer. She ran back into the house with the weapon, and they began to fight.

He punched her in the stomach, so she shot across the bedroom like a bullet. He slapped her so hard, her mouth filled with blood. But the whole time she held on to the machete. In front of the stove, she planted her feet and swung it at him. He looked at her, amazed, as the blade cut through his neck and his head went flinging into the sink. Covered with green goo that had come shooting out of his ears, she ran over to the faucet to look at the head, and she saw that it was crying. 'I love you,' the head said. 'I love you too,' she answered, sobbing. And then, still weeping, she flicked on the garbage disposal."

"Jesus," Blessica says.

My mother drinks from her glass. "So, that's a very sad story, eh? But so what? Because today, as I sit here drinking this lovely vino, and looking at you two gorgeous boys, I can laugh at this fairy tale because I'm happy. I'm so full of smiles because Tomás, and you, Cecil, are much more lucky than the stupid girl and the zombie husband. Because you have real love, not the fake love that is really hate, or something forced on you because you are poor. You love each other, maybe forever, and that's a precious thing that not everybody in this life can say. Today, your hearts break to pieces because you can't be in each other's arms. But when this finally is over, and we're all still hopefully alive, I promise you that you'll kiss each other again and whisper sweet words into each other's ears. So I want you to remember that no matter what your mamis or daddy says, what the school says, what anybody says, you have this precious, precious love that nobody can take from you. Your love makes you strong. That's all that matters."

Both boys are crying. Their shoulders shake. Large tears drip from their faces. Their mouths hang open. They clutch the plates in their laps.

My mother weeps into her hands. Paul walks over to Tomás

and kisses his cheek. I rush to them and hug them both. My mother comes over and hugs Paul and me, and her whole body trembles.

I look at Blessica and Cecil. Blessica has gone to her son and embraced him. Cecil clings onto her arms. He presses his eyes into her shoulder and sobs.

Like me, Blessica doesn't cry. She kisses the crown of her son's head. Her pretty face goes haggard with worry.

"I'm sorry," she says, kissing him again. "I'm so sorry."

Later, after we've all cleaned up after the party and it's time to turn in, Paul and I check on our son before lights out. Tomás lies in bed, folding his hands behind his head. A blue-and-white calculus book splays open on the floor. The bed's headboard radiates a corona of Cecil's pinned-up poems and drawings. Tomás stares at the ceiling, his face tense and unreadable. I want to ask if he's finished his homework but manage to muzzle myself.

"Hey, buddy," Paul says, picking up the calculus book and putting it on the nightstand.

"This is the hardest thing I've been through in my life," Tomás replies.

Paul and I exchange glances.

"It's not always going to be this way," I say.

Tomás's lips tense into a line. "I don't think that anyone can understand what I'm going through." He pauses. "What kids my age are going through."

"Well, son, maybe your mother and I can understand a little bit," Paul says.

I sit on the bed, touching Tomás's arm. Paul caresses the back of my neck. Tears roll down the sides of Tomás's face. I stretch out my sleeve and dab them away from his cheeks, his jaw, and his throat.

"It feels like the end of everything," our son says. "Like we don't even have a chance. Before, when you guys were young, things were still okay. Like you thought that you could have a good life. A long life. A safe life. Go to college. Get a job. Be with somebody. Have a future. But I don't have that. Like, kids my age, we don't have that.

"I'm just worried about everything all the time. Every day, every minute. About getting shot or getting choked by some cop putting his knee on me. Getting trapped in a fire. Losing you, because you're old, and if you got sick with it, you could die. And I love you guys, but the only person who really understands me is him. My boyfriend. Who I can't touch. Who I can't talk to alone, in person. Who I can't be with. And I'm so lonely. I feel dead. Like, will I never be with him again? Because I can't live like that. I won't live like that. I can't. I can't. I can't live like this anymore."

"Yes, you can," I say. "You have to."

"No." Tomás's face tightens into a wet clump.

"Honey," I say.

"Mom," my son says.

"Baby, we're going to get through this," Paul tells him in a shredded voice.

Tomás goes quiet for a long time.

"I just wanted you to know," he finally says, "how it is for me. Because I'm so scared. And sometimes it feels like he's the only thing that's keeping me alive."

Tomás brushes off his tears with his forearm. His breath comes in harsh gusts. I lean over and hug his torso, gripping him while his ribs jerk beneath my cheek.

That night, neither Paul nor I can sleep. At one in the morning, he gets up from bed and disappears into his study. I stay under the covers for another hour until I, too, realize that I'll remain awake. No sounds come from Tomás's room. I look out the window. The sky shines as tawny as an owl feather from the smoke and light pollution.

I reach under the bed, wriggling my fingers until I feel the cool metal edge of my computer. I raise its lid, turn it on. Entering a block of files, I open *A History of Hazardous Objects*. I click through until I find the photograph I'm looking for. It shows a white woman in her mid-thirties. She lies in her bed, only partially covered. The blankets fold back to reveal her upper body. She wears an open, striped nightgown and a bra. A white man in a tweed blazer—a doctor— stands above her and pulls the front hem of the nightgown away from her torso. He reveals a huge oval bruise that stretches from her left hip to her stomach. Her eyes are closed. Her arm bends from her shoulder at an awkward angle. Her hand curves outward, as if she'd like to shield herself. I remember how my mother said I drew well as a child, and I poke around in my nightstand drawer for a notebook and a pencil. I spend some time sketching the woman's figure, stony face, and the dark stain spreading across her hip. I'm drawing Ann Hodges, the only human known to be hit by a meteorite.

The pain I feel over my son's heartbreak lifts slightly when I finish my copy of the photo. I look at the woman's bruise in my drawing, and then on the screen, wondering at the strange and terrible thing she went through. Most meteorites touch down without any verification at all. The great majority of rocks crash in the middle of the ocean or the wastes of the deserts. Observed incidents remain rare sources of data, if researchers manage to document witnesses' recountings through on-site interviews, as in the case of Leonid Kulik. Still, even then, an eyewitness can typically only describe seeing a flash in the sky, or hearing and feeling the *ka-thunk* of a sonic boom. We have very little record of the behaviors of meteorites as they reach terra firma. Nor, except in the unique case of Ann Hodges, do we know much of these cataclysms' potential influence on the human psyche.

I begin to type:

The story of the Hodges Meteorite offers another important chapter in the history of NEO impacts, as this event teaches us the outsized and traumatic effects that meteorite contacts might have on human populations. The incident, as famous as it is today, began much the same as other, far more typical sightings of bolides and fireballs. At 5:28 pm on Tuesday, November 30, 1954, hundreds of people across eastern Alabama reported seeing a bright red object that streaked through the sky. It traveled at approximately thirty thousand miles per hour. As NASA later learned, the object broke off from a chondrite asteroid that weighed as much as one hundred fifty pounds, but most of its matter evaporated upon entry into the atmosphere, leaving a stony fusion of stardust and particles that amounted to no more than the size of a house cat. While Alabamans screamed at the flash and ran to their phones to report an air strike perpetrated by the Communists, Mrs. Ann Hodges lay drowsing on her sofa in her home in the small town of Sylacauga. . . .

Ann sweated and murmured beneath her blanket as the meteor snapped in the sky like a body's last nerve. Still innocent of the great workings above her, she attempted to sleep away the heavy sensation that spread through her limbs whenever she looked into her future and couldn't see the laughing lark of a girl she had once been.

Ann's mother, Ida Franklin, sewed quietly in the next room. On account of Ann's feeling poorly (and she felt poorly so often these days), Ida had arrived early in the morning to cook breakfast for her daughter's husband, Eugene Hodges, a utility contractor who looked away from Ann whenever she piped up at the pastor after Sunday services or guffawed in the movie house.

Don't make such a spectacle of yourself, he would say to his wife afterward. Why do you have to be such a clack-box?

Any time he spoke to her in this manner, Ann would feel all the muscles in her face trembling, as if she'd walked out into the cold without any clothes on.

Marriage is a girl's dream and a woman's burden, Ida liked to tell Ann when she complained. Your job is to make him happy, even if you don't feel any perkier than a pig who's just learned about ham.

Now Ann rested on the sofa, drifting away from her cares. Suddenly, she heard a whistle; a flap in the air. A nine-pound piece of the meteorite blasted like a grenade through the roof of her house. It ricocheted off her Philco radio console and slammed into her left hip.

Ann! Ida screamed.

The house filled with dust and smoke.

Ann lay on the floor, her pelvis twisting. Her eyes stared

blankly through the fumes. She didn't feel the pain, yet. Her body lacked any sensation at all.

Momma.

My baby, my baby! Ida chanted.

Ann felt her mother's arms reach around her shoulders. She saw a hole in the ceiling. Ida kissed Ann all over her face, in a way she hadn't done since Ann was a small child.

Ann looked across the room. A large rock smoked on her blackened carpet.

She closed her eyes. Her mind wafted, the same as the dust that swirled overhead in gusts and pretty patterns.

She felt herself vomiting even as a deep, delicate sensation enveloped her. She wanted to float like that for a long time.

But men came.

Ann opened her eyes. Other husbands from the neighborhood crowded into her living room. They lifted her, tenderly, taking care of her.

One, two, three, *up!*

The stalwarts carried her across the house, to her bedroom. She saw their angelic faces smiling down. She levitated with happiness.

Aren't you boys so sweet to help me, she whispered, feeling their warm hands cradle her throbbing body.

The men brought her to bed. They lay her down, gently. She watched them bustle around, jabbering, while the afternoon flowed over her and the light slowly softened. She pressed her hand to her damaged flesh and knew herself anointed.

Outside her window, she could see people gossiping and staring. One man wore spectacles and had a camera slung around his neck; he scratched at a pad of paper with a pencil.

Her own husband, his face red and frantic, pushed his way through the crowd. He barreled into the bedroom, shouting, What in the hell!

Got ourselves a situation, going to have to call the Pentagon, one of the men explained. Could be the Russkies.

Ann, get up, enough of this nonsense Eugene barked.

Ann smiled at him through her tears. *We had a little excitement here today,* she sighed.

A doctor ran in and shushed them. He lifted her slip. The
men ogled her white-and-purple hip as the pain deepened
down to her bone. She felt it make her special. The doctor gave
her medicine while the photographers' flashbulbs sparkled
outside her windows like tiger eyes in the dark.

A man in uniform entered the room. He'd wrapped the rock
in one of her bathroom towels and carried the parcel in both
hands.

Going to have to get this tested, she heard him say.

Might need to ask the landlord for permission first, Eugene
said.

Army doesn't need permission from anybody, the man in
the uniform said.

You can't take it, it's mine, Ann replied, dreamily. *God intended it for me. After all, I'm the one it hit.*

My hands rest on the keyboard. I read what I've written, twice,
three times. As in the case of the Kulik business, this isn't what
NASA had in mind when it assigned me to author part of the
action plan. The majordomos overseeing the administration of
funds will wonder why they're reading about Ann Hodges's nervous collapse instead of a clear précis offering statistical break-
downs of impacts that have affected urban vs. rural areas, and
terra firma sites vs. those in the ocean.

I must be having writer's block, I tell myself. Or the fire and
pandemic have given me some sort of psychological issue. I've
always associated the act of storytelling with an inability to say,
directly, what your problem is, either because you have a sadness

so bad it's ruined your hopes or you're too scared to name the cause of your fear. Ever since I heard about Brother Death, I've rejected yarns and legends in favor of the rational path that led me to radar astronomy, with its careful measuring of an object's diameter, its brightness, and the distance of its close approaches. Even when we find ourselves in ambiguous territory, which is often, astronomers don't waffle. We plug error estimates into our studies instead of leaving readers to clutch at an emotion or wonder at a metaphor. But as I read over my version of Hodges's story, I see that the supports I've used to prop up my life for the past forty years now seem to be slipping.

I'm tired, I realize. I don't want to think any more. I'm writing weirdly because of the stress. Forget about it, I tell myself. Have at it again tomorrow.

I close my computer and try to sleep.

Morning. As if by agreement, we don't eat as a family. Tomás quietly swallows a microwaved cheddar-cheese quiche at the kitchen table and doesn't answer any of my cautious questions before disappearing into the backyard. Paul takes a bagel into his office, and my mother drinks tea in the TV room. I wash up after snacking on leftover cassoulet and check our cupboards, seeing that we're low on most of our food staples. I only shop once a month now, if I can get away with it.

When I finish wiping down the counters, I stand still and listen to the pipe under the sink go *drip, drip, drip, drip.* How do you fix a dripping pipe? Not a single person in this house, I realize, has any notion, but bringing a plumber in here so that he or she can breathe all over us seems impossible. Google might have plumbing wisdom to share, but I'd be fine never looking at another screen in my life. It's 11 AM, and my brain feels dry after I've spent hours twisting my unsleeping body around my comforter when I wasn't writing my opus.

I open the cabinet beneath the sink and put a bowl under the pipe. Floor's wet. I mop up the water with a towel, step out of the kitchen. Besides fixing the drip or rewriting my report, I should be preparing for the trip that Somnang and I will take to Goldstone Observatory in a few days. Instead, I take laundry to the machines in the garage. I pull our wrinkled bedding from the dryer, which I or maybe even someone else should have done yesterday, and put it in a basket. I feed our shirts and jeans and underwear into the washer and fill its trap with detergent, then click it on. I pick up the basket with the clean sheets and take them into Tomás's bedroom. His calculus book remains on the nightstand in the exact same spot, and in the same orientation, as when Paul left it there last night. On top of his bed, his computer is open, and I peer at the screen but see only poetry that I don't want to read.

I put the basket on the floor and imagine myself hunting for my son throughout the house in order to capture him and march him to his bedroom so he can do the problems I gave him one or two weeks ago. Such a drama seems impossible considering the delicate emotional situation that we navigated yesterday, so I remove the computer, put it on his nightstand, and yank his covers off the bed. I strip the mattress and struggle to put on the clean bottom elasticized sheet, but it keeps slipping off, so I have to put my knee under the mattress so that I can get enough leverage to snap it on. My armpits begin perspiring. After that, I put on the blanket and the quilt and slip new pillowcases on the pillows and tidy the whole thing up so the bed looks nice. In Paul's and my bedroom, I repeat the process with our bed and nearly sprain my back when I try to lift up our mattress with my left knee.

Last night, when Tomás was crying in my arms, I felt like I'd die with love for my son and my mother and my husband, so it doesn't make sense if this extreme attachment to my family right now is getting bitten and chewed by a painful rage that rears up in me like a badger. On top of my dresser, I see a small blue glass vase that Paul and I bought in Venice in 1997, while at a conference that turned into a vacation full of laughter and sex and eating seafood by the glinting water. I don't know what's happening to me, but I can say with great confidence that there is a 78 percent chance that I'll smash that little vase if I don't distract myself. I turn away from the dresser so I can't see it.

My body and chest feel levitated and my head is stormy. Adrenaline? Menopause? Back in April my gynecologist, who examined me in her deserted office while dressed in Hefty garbage bags and blue vinyl gloves, took my blood pressure and told me that my resting heart rate (RHR) was 98, which was bad. She began talking about a possible cardiac event or lupus or thyroid failure but diagnosed me with anxiety in the end. My gynecologist believes in alternative medicine and so prescribed Zoom yoga and a series of deep breathing exercises whose choreographies I promptly forgot. She also told me to make sure I scheduled all my delayed women's-health tests and to keep an eye on my heart rate.

She explained that I could get an app on my phone that checked my RHR, and so I installed one. As I now pull my phone out of my sweatpants pocket, I see it represented on the screen as a small, red square with a white heart at the center of it, a white heart whose right half is scarred by parallel red lines, as if blood were dripping down, but I don't think this effect is intentional. Beneath the squared heart, it reads "cardio." I press "cardio" and my phone tells me to put my fingers on a bright light that shines on its back side. I do so and a few moments later learn that my RHR is 101.

I go to my bed and sit down and then lie down. Breathing in and out, in and out from the diaphragm, I hope that this ritual resembles the protocol prescribed to me by my gynecologist. My phone's still in my hand, and I press the Chrome button. I try to type "breathing exercises for stress" in the search bar, but I can't do this with my thumb and the text comes out mangled. Instead of pressing the little microphone so I can bawl out my search, I close my eyes and keep breathing. In and out, in and out, in and out.

When this doesn't work, I retrieve my computer and its power cord from beneath the bed and walk out of the bedroom. My phone says that it's 11:45. It seems that pandemic time runs slower and in a dumber way. I don't understand why I'm hating everything right now because I used to want my family to be around me almost constantly, and I also dreamed of having a magical power that would make the clock stop without obliterating all life.

I walk over to Paul's and my office. I open the door without knocking, because if this is really my co-office now, I should just be able to enter. I find my husband glaring at his computer screen, and he shakes his head at me without looking in my direction. That means that Paul is working on something very important and I shouldn't distract him. Mentally, I do now actually break the blue Venetian vase into tiny smithereens and stomp on the pieces with my heels. I turn around and walk back out.

I wander around the house with my computer under my moist armpit until I reach the living room, which is a dead space that, a decade ago, I decorated in a great burst of excitement. It has a green-beige sofa, a walnut coffee table, two floral paintings, and a blue-and-red Berber rug. I remember to do the deep breathing again as I look at the sofa and its small pink throw pillow. I bought that pillow in a Bed, Bath & Beyond because I worried that Paul and I weren't modeling healthy social practices for Tomás and should invite people for dinner parties and so on. Though this resolution faded almost as soon as I bought the pillow, which today connects to my pro-social aspirations in ways I can't quite piece together, I think I could begin living in the living room by commandeering it as a writing space. But, instead, I back away and head again to my son's room. He's there now, evidently, as my mother's standing in his doorway, laughing.

"That Blessica's a piece of work," she's saying.

"She's all right," Tomás says.

"When I get finished with her, she's sure as hell going to be eating your chili," Mom goes on.

"Oh, Grandma," Tomás says.

Mom smiles at me as I approach. I peer into Tomás's room to find him wearing an old T-shirt that says SUPREME and blue sweatpants, his feet bare and his laptop resting on his legs as he lies back on his great-looking bed. The calculus book remains in place on his nightstand, as if it's an insect born in an antediluvian era and is now preserved and motionless for all time in deathless amber.

"Hey, buddy, were you able to do those problems I gave you?" I ask.

Tomás waggles his head from shoulder to shoulder and presses the heels of his hands into the bed. He made this gesture, I remember, as a child. A burst of released love detonates beneath my sternum until he says, "I'm going to do them today."

"Okay," I say.

"I will," he says.

"Yes, all right."

"I'm going to do it, Mom."

"Okay." My eyes become hot and agitated.

"Laurita," my mother says.

"Yeah."

"Go take a nap."

"Okay." I turn and walk back down the hall, dropping the plug-in part of the computer's power cord on the floor and picking it up again.

Back in my bedroom, I throw the computer in the middle of the bed, yank back the covers, and crawl in. I stare at the ceiling, listening to my heart blasting. I should probably call my doctor, I think, studying the bumpy white paint that covers the walls, but instead sit up again. I put two shams against my back and one across my thighs. My computer feels solid in my hands. I bend down awkwardly and plug the power cord into the wall socket above the baseboard, nearly falling straight off the bed as I do so. I sit back up and balance the computer on my lap pillow.

Decades later, after the *Life* magazine cover, the lawsuits, the divorce, and the onset of kidney disease, Ann Hodges held tight to her faith that she was special.

She lay in her asylum bed and looked down at her body. She still had the scar. It was long and shiny. She could study it as if it were a line of scripture.

Still, she wished her mother were here. She wanted Ida to come back from the dead, to caress her face the way she had that afternoon the rock burst in through the roof.

Ann looked out at the large ward. Pretty nurses bustled down its aisles, dispensing pills.

I am Jesus Christ, said a woman with long, gray hair, as she took her medicine.

Yes, yes, the nurses agreed.

I want to leave this place, wept a skinny man with a face like an old rat's.

There, there.

I'm the only person in the world, Ann told a nurse with blue eyes.

Well, isn't that something! the nurse said, as she handed Ann three green capsules.

I'm the only person who's ever been touched by a star.

Swallow this down, now. You swallow it like a good girl.

Ann swallowed.

Eugene didn't understand, she explained. My mother,

neither. God sent me that piece of heaven. Because I couldn't live like that. I won't live like that. I can't. I can't. I can't live like that anymore.

You're going to be just fine, the nurse crooned. And in a jiffy, too.

The nurse walked away.

Ann shivered in her bed. She reached down to touch the feathered skin on her hip. The star had fallen onto her body, lifting her out of her mind as easily as any electric shock. She remembered when the reporters came to her, and the way the lights had warmed her face as the cameras clicked. The name "Mrs. Eugene Hodges" had appeared in the Alabama's *Birmingham Post-Herald* and even in Alaska's *Nome Nugget*. And she'd posed like Ava Gardner for her *Life* magazine cover. Her husband looked at her strangely as she chattered on and on about the miracle. People said getting marked by the star wasn't good for her nerves, and it was true that sometimes she couldn't quite understand why this blessing had come to her. All in all, the meteorite was a mystery that moved ahead of her always: huge, dazzling, and, as often as not, obstructing her view. She could never quite decipher the message it had burned into her. She could never see her way through it.

Yes, she couldn't see through it, to what it meant. There were nights, in the hospital, when she listened to the wailing of the patients and felt the old fear creep up again, making its way from her hip and crawling through the rest of her body. That's when Satan whispered to her that the star wasn't from God and if it meant anything at all, it only told the story of how Hell waited for us around every corner, every bend.

One day you'll be dead, and never again will men lift you in their arms like you're a little girl, Satan hissed. Never again will your mother caress your face like that.

But Ann would shut her ears to those lies. She'd look out the window, up to where the stars waited. You're the only ones who understand how it is for me, she prayed. Because I'm so scared. And sometimes, it feels like you're all that's keeping me alive.

My computer reads 3:35. I look out the window at the woolly afternoon light. My body feels less compressed, and when I press the red heart on my phone and push my finger to the light, my RHR reads 87.

I shouldn't have felt so mad at everyone before. It makes me ashamed. My mother must be right, and I should try to get some sleep. I put my computer back under the bed and push my head into the pillow. I try to drowse but my thoughts catch on Ann Hodges and that dark shadow streaking across her body.

Ann Hodges wasn't lucky like I am. Her husband abandoned her. She had no children. She lost control of her own mind. She was the victim of the most farfetched event, one that was predictable but at the same time unimaginable. Like plague. The contemporary news accounts explain that Hodges herself didn't die in a likely way. After the meteorite crashed through her roof, she didn't succumb to her injuries. Instead, she couldn't ever relax, ever find peace. She died of kidney failure at the age of 52, in a sanatorium not ten miles from the place where she was born, where she was treated for end-stage renal failure and extreme anxiety.

4

The Vanishing of the Dinosaurs

"I can't believe I've been walking around looking like a skunk for years," my mother says.

"You don't look like a skunk." I stand above her, holding scissors in my left hand.

"Then I look like I fell headfirst into a pot of Chinese White," she says.

"What's Chinese White?"

"A white paint, made with zinc." My mother's hands dance as she talks. "Very delicate. Very bright and smooth. When placed next to sap green, it's so wonderful you could cry. And when mixed with indigo, it makes a delicious baby blue."

I peer at her in the bathroom's floor-length mirror, which is affixed to the inside of the door. She sits in a chair that I dragged in from the dining room. Over her shoulders, she wears a white towel that I fastened in front of her throat with a steel clip that normally secures my printouts. I stand behind her. My scissors hover over her hair, which grows from her head pale and luminous but trails down to those crow-black ends that haven't seen a hairdresser in two years.

"You know, I could just re-dye it," I say. "Get rid of the gray."

"It is not gray. It's silver."

"Get rid of the silver."

"No, I don't think so. Because that is not who I am *now*."

"All right."

"Who I am now is glamorous, with hair like the moon and the eyes of a matador." She raises her chin to show off her cheekbones and eyeliner.

"Yes."

"It's a whole look. Like Georgia O'Keefe."

I begin snipping. The black locks fall to the floor in little commas.

"The reason I could not embrace who I *am* is because I was depressed," she says. "When you're depressed, you can be bald or a skunk head or fat and you don't care. Let me tell you, all the girls in the nursing home were like that, like dead."

I stop cutting. "It's not a nursing home. It's an assisted-living environment."

"Meh."

"And whenever we went over there you told us everything was great."

She raises one shoulder and drops it. "Oh, it wasn't so bad. I'm exaggerating."

I look at her in the mirror.

"It was the shits," she says.

"But you broke your leg and the doctor said—"

"Yakkety, yakkety, yakkety."

"Why didn't you say something?"

"Because, I *know*. You think I didn't want to kill my own mother a million times?"

"It's not like that with us."

"Yeah, but you put me in that dump, and so what?" Mom says softly.

I squeeze my eyes shut. I feel sick to hear this, even though I've known it for a while. "Sorry!"

"No need to be upset. You're a good girl." She raises a long, elegant finger that glitters with a new scarlet nail polish that must have arrived in one those boxes and envelopes that now form a daily obstacle on our front steps. "You don't have to worry about your old mama, and even if you did, I wouldn't tell you about all of my sufferings anyways because I always protect you from bad things."

I snip the black hair on the right side of her face until the first signs of a bob appear.

"Mmmmmm," she says, modeling in the mirror.

I gently move my hands through her hair, almost caressing her while I work.

"Yes, I was depressed," she goes on, "and so I didn't think I was good enough for fashion, for wine, for loving life, for the Chinese White and the greens, the reds, the yellows, the purples, the blues, the browns, the pinks, the oranges, all that."

I continue cutting.

"But now I am going to be Georgia O'Keefe, and guess what, lady, I am never moving out of this house. Except that as soon as this pinche virus thing is over, I'm going to travel to Italy and paint there, for like a year."

"Sounds good," I say.

The rest of the black hair begins to mount at my feet. While I work, Mom tugs up the tender skin around her jowls and talks of buying turquoise jewelry, black caftans like Louise Nevelson used to wear, rebozos like Frida Kahlo's, and putting on a red lip, which will be her new special signature. The silver bob takes shape until it frames her face with soft and shining light. I wet my fingers at the sink's tap and fluff out the strands, making small, smooth waves. I undo the clip and whisk off the towel with a flourish. I gaze at her reflection, marveling. She is intensely, excruciatingly, beautiful. Meanwhile, she continues to swivel her head back and forth and explain that in Italy, she will paint the Arno and get a lover.

An hour later, I'm lying in bed and trawling newly published medical-journal articles on the web, which I shouldn't do because I was just happy in the bathroom with my mother. The rest of my family doesn't waste the morning: Paul teaches in his office, Mom has gone back to painting in the TV room, and Tomás does homework in his bedroom. He had better be doing his homework. This semester, my son takes AP Calculus, AP English, AP History, AP Chemistry, and Honors Biology. He should be studying for the ACT. Before COVID, he belonged to the Science Society, the Creative Writing Club, Chess Club, he was on soccer, and he volunteered at Habitat for Humanity. It was a perfect Caltech application in the making, and now it's getting blown up into safety school fodder.

I poke around until I find studies on the impacts that COVID will have on gifted children. A recent article in *Psychological Trauma* reports that the cognitive hazards adolescents face come mainly from the people who love them best. The study's authors write, with hilarious understatement, about a boom in *parental psychopathology* during the pandemic. They predict this crisis will lead to a worldwide decline in children's mental health and academic performance, as well as a simultaneous spike in behavioral disorders. These developments will usher in a cascade of disasters, they intimate, catastrophes that include unemployment, workplace accidents, the rise of early-death rates and suicide, high crime, teen pregnancy, economic recessions, runaway inflation, world wars, and other things that mothers will inevitably be held responsible for causing.

I knock my computer off my knees and burrow into the bed.

A heavy, thick weight descends on my face and my chest and my stomach and my legs as I lie on my back. This sensation of sinking down to the depths of the earth emanates from my state of mind, I realize, but it feels as if I've grown denser, rapidly, like a white dwarf before it explodes into a supernova. During the worst months of Paul's illness, my panic kept me thin and rapid. But my core now grows so heavy that it can't endure its own gravitational force. "When you're depressed, you can be bald or a skunk head or fat and you don't care," I hear my mother say in my head. Still, depression and related weight gain are normal reactions to a global crisis, I read in recent issues of *The New York Times*. The *Times* also says that the cure for pandemonium is something called *self-care*. I attempt to follow the newspaper's instructions by tucking my hand under my sweatshirt. I rub my fattening breasts and belly. When that doesn't work, I stick my hand beneath my sweatpants and pat my big bush.

When lockdown first began, Paul and I became briefly erotically excited. The stay-at-home order presented itself initially as a benefit of the apocalypse. We happily submitted to a cosmic morality lesson that appeared to reimpose a set of ancient values. These tenets hold that people should spend quality time with their families and cease distracting themselves with frivolities like consumerism and careers. In the first two months, Paul and I celebrated this altered state by having sex more often, at strange, daylight hours. Here, on this mattress, we grabbed at each other and stifled our moans by pressing our mouths on each other's shoulders. In other words, we were terrified and that terror put a spring in our step. I displayed other industrious behaviors, such as journaling and meditating and insisting that we all eat together every night at the table. Also the cleaning. But now, the collapse of the planet from all sides doesn't make me want to journal or even touch myself. I don't want anything except for perfect sanitation and survival, because if you're afraid for too long, your inner emotional technology snaps off. My own personal hedonic processor exploded months ago. Wires and smoke are coming out of it.

Beep.

I turn my computer toward me and toggle onto my email. My supervisor, Somnang, has sent me a brief message:

Remember gng to Goldstone for Apophis scan Mon next week meet you there at 10 am

I curl into a fetal position. Getting out of the house and going to Goldstone will be good for me. I think it's funny that radar-imaging a potentially world-destroying asteroid will be healing. I laugh into my pillow, big, strange chuckles and guffaws that would alarm my family if they could see me doing this. I remember to remind myself that I'm grateful. This makes me stop laughing. There are people out there dying on ventilators. There is a thing called long COVID. We don't even have it, or we don't think that we've had it. Actually, maybe we've all had it and don't know that we had it, and in two years we'll all die from blood clots.

I get out of bed. In the bathroom, I wash my hands. I go out to the hall and pass Paul's office. He lowers his face toward his keyboard. He types angrily with two fingers and then looks up.

"Can you read a draft?" he asks. "I'm going to send it to *Nature*."

"Email it to me."

My mother's laughter floats over the cries emanating from her television. I dither for a moment in the hallway, looking at her drawings of roses. Each one is formed out of a black line of varying thickness, which curves and coils in mad tangles. I see that she was right when she had looked at my work notebook and said, "You're making roses like me." My sketches of satellite routes are rigid versions of these maps of disassembled flowers, which are also like the silhouettes of exploding stars, the hoof prints made by a crazed horse as it races back and forth across the snow, or the desperate path of a woman as she runs around the house to escape her violent husband. I trace one of the roses with my fingertips until I begin to feel nervous.

Stop it, I think. *Get it together. You have to whip this place and your family into shape.*

I move toward Tomás's room. His door is closed. I knock briefly, and, when no response arrives, I quickly prepare a lecture on the importance of doing homework. I will tell him about the study in *Psychological Trauma* and the risk of drug addiction and teen pregnancy—the latter of which is actually not pertinent, thank God—and the incipient economic recession. If he still insists on loafing, I'll sit on him with my actual, literal bottom until he begins to do the bonus calculus problems that I assigned him maybe now a month ago.

I enter the room. Tomás sits on his bed reading a paperback book. It's Camus's *The Plague.* Tomás's mouth stiffens as he reads. He looks like a stranger. The way his lips turn down is new. He glares up at me with his father's large eyes.

"You're okay, baby," I say. "You're doing great."

I shut the door.

Since we're going to be out of food soon, it's time for me to shop. I drive to Trader Joe's. The storefront presents a rock-face exterior overhung by a huge red and white sign. I park and walk toward the entrance after fixing my mask's loops over my ears. Approaching a vertical stack of metal shopping carts, I pull one out while a tall, bulky man waits his turn behind me. He wears a red cotton bandana over the lower part of his face and stands approximately four feet away. I struggle with the cart as he steps forward. Studies show that bandanas don't offer the same protection as double-ply surgical masks, like the one that I'm wearing. A person wearing a bandana instead of a proper mask and standing within four feet of me isn't trying hard enough.

"Do you need help?" he asks kindly.

"No thank you." I jerk the cart out and roll it toward him. "There you go."

"Oh, thanks!" His eyes squint and his bandana widens, indicating that he smiles beneath it.

"Sure thing." I smile back too, though I'm not sure if he can see it.

I get my own cart and take my place in a twelve-person line, making sure that another customer in a real mask stands between me and the bandana wearer. We're all looking at our phones. It's September 18, at 11:32 AM. The evacuation warning remains in effect: The Bobcat Fire has now destroyed 60,557 acres and remains only 15 percent contained. Also, someone named Amy Dorris has accused President Trump of sexually assaulting her in 1997. *He just shoved his tongue down my throat and I was pushing him off,* she's quoted as saying in *The Guardian. And then that's when his grip became tighter and his hands were very gropey and all over my butt, my breasts, my back, everything.* The line eventually pushes forward, and I enter the store.

My list is: milk, celery, tomatoes, bottled water, chicken breasts, cereal, toilet paper, fresh tomatoes, kale, and cilantro for the family; frozen burritos for my upcoming trip to Goldstone; and Milanos and butterscotch ice cream for my mother. The aisles jostle with people who mutely grab loaves of bread and jars of olives. Unlike the horror period of March and April— when the shelves held little more than empty plastic bags and I stood in the canned goods section with my arms flapping at my sides and my head rapidly expanding with the helium of fear— the shop now bursts with food and paper products. Everyone walks up and down the rows at a normal pace, except for a small red-headed boy who's just torn off his face-covering while his empty-eyed mother pulls on his arm. It's impossible to maintain the six-foot rule here. Is it six feet with masks or six feet only without masks? Can you get it from six-year-olds or eight-year-olds? I should know this by now. I idle behind my cart until the mother hauls her child off in the direction of produce.

In dairy, the tubs of ice cream beckon from their cold cages. Some people, I notice, wear spaceman-looking face shields with no masks beneath. Others wear just a regular good mask in the right way and some people with masks wear them under their noses. By the cereals, I find the man with the red bandana. He forms a cabal of other negligent bandana wearers, three by my count. One white woman with long brown hair stares at racks of red wine like they're her boyfriends while slothfully wearing a mask beneath her lower lip. Then there's a white man with rimless glasses in the frozen aisle section who wears no mask at all. I sidle up carefully and snatch six cheese burritos, a special junk food that Somnang and I enjoy eating when we're in the field. The maskless man breathes all over everything and I scoot away. I don't understand why vigilantes aren't toppling him to the ground.

At checkout, I look down at my feet, examining my cold and unpedicured toes in their sandals. Blue tape marks on the floor indicate the space that should exist between each customer, but everyone ignores them. A masked Brown woman stands about three feet ahead of me with her eyes closed and a cart stuffed with beer and frozen pizza. She doesn't express fear or anger at my closeness, but, even if she did, I can't stand farther away because two feet behind me is a young white man wearing a mask and texting. It can take between two to five to fourteen days for symptoms to develop. Symptoms include a sore throat and neurological mayhem.

"*No, I won't, I WON'T, I WON'T, I WON'T*," everybody hears a child yelling, back around the produce section.

The masked checkout girl behind the plastic partition is small, dark, Latina, and looks as if a giant vacuum has depleted her of all vitamins and minerals. As she bags my selections with plastic-gloved hands, she stoops and dark shadows smolder under her eyes. She puts the bags in my cart, and when she somehow reads my expression, she winks at me.

"It's only the end of the world," she says.

"Oh, look at all the people, it's so nice," my mother says.

It's evening. The two of us are walking through the streets of Pasadena. That is, I walk while pushing my mother's wheelchair, which I've retrieved from the garage. The city has banned automobiles on several roads so residents with cabin fever can amble around the suburbs without fear of being hit by cars. People I've never seen before stroll down the asphalt. As a male stranger walks toward us, his black curly hair springs from the sides of his head like the flaps of a deerstalker hat. He nods at us, and my mother waves. The stranger wears a mask with an army-fatigues print, so that I wonder, not for the first time, if there must be some masculinity problem with wearing cloth over the nose and the mouth. A young couple wearing matching black masks passes us after him. The girl's shoulders slope inward, and she wraps her thin hands around the arm of her boyfriend, who sports a pony-tail and talks about Trump while she listens. They nod hello too. My mother waves again. A blond maskless woman strides toward us, holding the leash of a gleaming Irish setter, whose gold and russet fur bounces around its neck. This woman edges her gaze away. Usually only Latino gardeners are visible in this neighborhood. If all goes well, we'll shrink back into our houses and likely never do this again. Meanwhile, my mother smiles at the woman with the Irish setter, even as the woman pretends not to see us.

I feel displaced, as if I'm another version of the person who's married to Paul, gave birth to Tomás, and works at JPL. I don't know everything about myself, I realize, even at this age. Gripping the handles of my mother's chair, I marvel at this superimposed hour, which seems like an alternative swapped in when we weren't looking. If the pandemic had never happened, I'd have finished a dry and succinct summation of the history of hazardous objects by now and be in my office, composing an article on the Yarkovsky drift, or a revised shape model for Apophis's orbit, or the hydration states of X-class asteroids. Or, I guess, I could be anywhere else at all.

While I steer my mother, I imagine a vast host of possible Lauras, who all bear different destinies as they circulate around an arrow pointing forward in time. I used to believe I was in control of these potential women and that my choices would dictate which among them would force their way to the front. That I have no more say about what the future holds than does a clam or a blade of grass or a teacup or a moth should be a relief, since that means I've been working way too hard and can just take a break. But the idea doesn't make me feel any better. The vortex of possible Lauras gets mingled, in my mind, with a scattering of Pauls and Tomáses and Moms, until the world itself, complete with a constellation of flying Irish setters, lifts off in a swirl of maybes. Some red setters go home and eat pork chops or dry packaged chow, while others spend the afternoon chasing balls that land in indistinguishably different arrangements. A percentage break free of their leashes and run off to Montebello or Glendale. At least one flies to the moon and dies like Laika, the Russian mutt launched into space on *Sputnik 2*.

"Makes you think," Mom says.

"Sorry, what?"

"Makes you think, I said."

"What, about the virus?"

"About how he is. In all of this. If he's still alive."

"Who's 'he?'"

"You-know-who."

"My dad?"

My mother doesn't answer.

"Mom, why are you thinking of him?"

I look down at my mother's hair, which she's combed neatly to the side. She's put on a black sweater, and on her fingers she wears silver and turquoise rings that I brought her back from a conference in Santa Fe. She folds her hands in her lap and emanates serenity as we watch the people move in little huddles or take awkward side steps to avoid each other.

"Sometimes you look back and you can't believe the things that you've done," is all she says.

Three days have passed since my walk with my mother, and now it's cocktail hour in the desert. In this cleansing heat, and under this long clear sky, I could almost believe that COVID doesn't exist. I sit with Somnang in the shade of DSS-14, Goldstone's 70-meter antenna, in Barstow. We splay out in metal-and-plastic lawn chairs, which Somnang has placed about three feet apart. With our masks slung beneath our chins, we sip Limoncello he brought in a thermos and eat my microwaved burritos. DSS-14 rises from the Mojave sands with its huge chalk-colored dish tilted toward invisible stars. The desert stretches out before us, parched and golden. The kilned air seeps into our bodies, loosening the muscles as the sun tumbles. Somnang and I spent all day programming data and receiving readings of Apophis, my old enemy. Already, we've mapped several images of Roy Tucker's asteroid, whose shape roughly approximates that of a titanic peanut. Our current best guesses estimate that it's composed of iron and a green crystalline substance called olivine. Right now, Apophis hurtles toward Earth at an exceptional, but safe, flyby of several million kilometers. Our current concern is its return trip in 2068.

For the past ten hours, we worked side by side while observing the dress and dance of safety protocols: masks, gloves, the minuet of physical distance, and, where possible, ventilation. Similarly, at the beginning of this little party, we held the thermos by a paper towel we tore from a big roll that sits at our feet and ate with our face coverings half on. After one or two refills of our drinks, Somnang removed his shoes and slipped the loops off his ears. I also felt myself decompressing or deflating. My past few months of hyperactive germ warfare suddenly look strange, almost demented, when reflected in the bottom of my glass. Out here in the desert, it feels as if my sense of reality has jammed its gears, like a bicycle that I crashed but still have to ride. I tell myself that lounging with Somnang in the fresh air isn't nearly as dangerous as grocery shopping or being in the hospital. And I know that Somnang hasn't socialized since March. And neither of us has any symptoms.

"These numbers," he says, watching a masked tech worker walking into the antenna.

I click my tongue. "Not the best."

"We'll see when we get back. Check and double-check."

"I thought Apophis was long put to bed."

"Not just yet. But better not fret about it now. There's always more data coming in."

"Yes."

Somnang unfurls his body in his chair as if he's been trapped in a trunk. "So, here we are again. Nice to be back, in any event."

"It's the first good work I've done in months. Haven't been able to concentrate."

"How's your report coming?"

I take a bite of burrito. "Badly."

"Everything's bad this year."

We both go quiet. The sun crawls across the desert. Somnang stares at the barrens, absentmindedly pushing at his lower lip with his fingers.

"You all right?" I ask.

He widens his eyes. "Oh, I don't know really."

"It's the pandemic."

"Ye-es."

"Eat some more, it'll soak up the alcohol."

"And what would the good of that be?"

"Just have a little bit."

Somnang takes a small chomp of the burrito before grabbing the thermos. He heaves himself up out of his chair and refills my glass, after which he pours two huge glugs into his. He drinks.

"You and Paul seem so very happy," he says after a while. "You two and the boy."

"Tomás."

"That's wonderful."

"Just so long as everyone stays alive, I'll be all right."

"Yes, of course. . . . And his health?"

"Paul's? They say he's good, but they also say, 'We'll see.' He's getting more tests in three months."

"I suppose that's all one can hope for in some situations."

"Seems like."

Somnang lifts the corners of his lips. "You know, Laura, I'll bet you never did a wrong thing in your whole life."

"What do you mean?"

"Only making an observation."

"Of course I have."

"No, but really."

I rub the space between my eyebrows, as if trying to erase something. "I put my mother in a nursing home."

"That's nothing." Somnang wrinkles up his face. "You're like some sort of . . . *elf*."

I laugh. "What the hell do you mean?"

"That you should never change. That you should keep being good." He scratches his hair, so that it stands straight up around his ears. "It's the best way."

"All right."

"Really, I wish I'd been good all my life. So does my wife." He pauses. "My ex-wife."

"You've never talked about her before."

"Annabeth Vong, who kept my last name. Out of spite."

"What happened?"

"I was an imperfect husband. Worked too hard. Among other failings."

"Somnang, we all work too hard."

"She said it was an obsession, chasing Near-Earthers. 'It won't bring back the dead,' she'd tell me. 'You can't go back and save the world.'"

"I don't understand."

"Oh, my brother. He died. Phnom Penh. 1975. He was one of Sak Sutsakhan's men." Somnang looks down, frowning. "Am I making sense?"

I smile at him. "I don't know."

"Anyway, after he was killed, and even after I married Annabeth, I lived to do this job." Somnang picks up the thermos again and pours more into both our glasses.

"Last one for me," I say.

"Just destined for the profession, I think. Since leaving Cambodia, I can't remember when I haven't been studying these things." He waves his hand up at the antenna. "Talking about them. Writing about them. Worrying about them. It made it impossible for me to be the right kind of man for Annabeth. Because she wanted what most women, people, want. I gave her a baby, but that just made everything worse. The truth is, *this* just interested me more than anything else on earth, and I should never have gotten married. Some people shouldn't. They have something lacking in them. Or, maybe that's not right. I wanted to give everything to my work. Thought it was the right choice. And it was. In some ways, at least."

As dusk falls across the dunes, he looks away from me, expressionless, almost as if he's forgotten I'm here.

"And then, I had some other . . . friendships. With people I thought might understand. In the end, though, everyone is the same. Forgive me for saying so, but every woman on this planet is exactly identical. And that's why I can say with perfect certainty that, when it came to Annabeth, the real problem was my absence, that I was never really *there*. I thought she was being unreasonable. I didn't realize that there was some sort of moral test in all of it. Not until the breaking point. When she began crying in such a way that it didn't seem normal. She was holding our daughter, Dara, and it seemed like she, my wife, was dying. It was terrifying. I tried to fix things then. Too late. She took the girl and moved away. I thought I might sue for custody, but then I remembered how Einstein trampled all over his women and children, and I thought, well, maybe I'm just of that species that isn't cut out for family life.

"I saw my daughter, though, on many occasions, bringing gifts, taking her out to dinner. But my wife has succeeded in stealing her. Every time I visited my child, it was all bitterness and morose silence. Until Dara finally admitted that she didn't want anything to do with me. Because of how I'd treated them, she said. That I was cold. Inhuman. It was a shock. To hear her say that showed me that my daughter had been deprived of any wish for a normal relationship with her own family. And she has no sister, no brother.

"All of this is such a loss to her, whatever she thinks of it now. Because a person does need people around them with whom they belong and share memories, who might teach them and love them. She must have grown up with such a chilly sense of the world. And I understood, on our last meeting, what I had done to her." His mouth flinches. "But that's how evil works, isn't it? No one sets out to do wrong. We just follow our natures."

He looks at his glass with reddening eyes.

"I suppose that later I'll regret saying all of this. Seems as if I've been by myself for too long."

"It's okay."

I reach for the roll of paper towels and give Somnang a clean sheet. He thanks me and dabs his face. We both grow silent again under the darkening sky. Purple shadows float above the sand and the rocks. DSS-14 looms above us like a giant flower. The trouble with Apophis suddenly seems to flatten its ears and recede into the gloaming. I want to fill the stillness with talk about how Somnang isn't evil, that people break up, that parenting is impossible, and that I'm not as good as I might seem. But I know better than that, at least.

When I've finished my work with Somnang, I drive back on the 15. I don't want to think of the data that he and I uncovered about Apophis. The highway stretches ahead under the clouds. The dry fields dash by, the roadside weeds and flowers a quick blur and the far-off red and yellow barns barely moving at all. The parallax effect. Cars zip past. Sometimes drivers wear masks, even with their windows rolled up. I'm drinking a Coke I bought at a McDonald's. On the radio, I hear songs that I never listened to when I was young but that come from my youth. The Cure. Erasure. Yaz. When I was a child, I was too busy with science to be interested in pop music, but I like it now.

The Bobcat Fire can't be seen from here. The sky gleams like a silver shield as I race on home.

The pipe under the sink's still an issue. It's two o'clock in the afternoon, and I'm in the kitchen, tucking my head and shoulders into the sink's cupboard to stare at the iron elbow and the water it leaks into the little bowl I put under the plumbing. The water has spilled over the rim and puddled on the bottom of the cabinet, staining it. I empty the bowl, sop up the moisture with a sponge, and wait until I can see the place in the joint where the liquid seeps through. I remember I put some electric tape in the hall closet a few years ago. I find only screwdrivers and Scotch Tape and a broom and rags there, though. I look in the bathroom junk drawer and the junk drawer in the foyer table and peek around my mother's bedroom and find nothing.

Paul doesn't know where anything is, he says, when I poke my head into his study, and when he offers to help, I say no. In the garage, I rummage around old shoes and books and find a roll of the silver stuff in a half-smashed box. Another fifteen minutes is spent looking for scissors, and then I'm back under the sink, cutting tape and wrapping it around the pipe. As I press the sticky stuff over the leak, I have a moment of clarity when I realize that it's possible I'm having a breakdown. I cut more tape from the roll, resolving that I'll finish my report tonight. I strap the tape on. It holds. It looks good. Just to make sure, I get the bowl that I'd used to protect the cabinet floor and put it back under the pipe. I get up and close the cupboard. As the little door latches, I hear a drop striking the bowl again.

I breathe and go to the refrigerator. The act of reaching into the cool bright rectangle reminds me of how my mother used to cook for me when I was a kid. She stood in our small kitchen with a cigarette in her mouth, unwrapped ground meat, and fried it before dousing it with spaghetti sauce. She inexplicably titled this dish "Hawaiian Meat." "Who wants some Hawaiian Meat?" "Hawaiian Meat is very expensive and good for you." "Eat your Hawaiian Meat." Uncapping the bottle of Ragù, she yelled at me about the nutritional and class-status benefits of Hawaiian Meat when she wasn't hollering about the lizard who thought it was a dragon until it tried to fly, or the girl who got her butt pinched by a cafeteria manager and turned into a man-eating Godzilla. I'd look up from my book as I sat at the plastic kitchen table, and then I'd look back down again. When she gave me my plate, I ate my meat and closed my eyes and imagined that I was at the ocean side, doing the hula and wearing a necklace of flowers.

I grab kale, chicken breasts, fresh tomatoes, and cilantro. Olive oil from the upper shelf of the cupboard; onions and garlic and lentils from the lower. I can cook double for dinner and freeze the leftovers. I don't make Hawaiian Meat. My recipe is a messy mix of ideas I've learned from healthy-cooking sites, some of them nerve-pinchingly alarmist, as they frighten the home chef with descriptions of the carcinogenic dangers of trans fats, factory-farmed chicken, grilled meats, wine, and other things that feel and taste good. From the drawer beneath the utensils, I get a large frying pan. A few dashes of olive oil gleam on the steel and I turn up the heat. I stand over the chicken breasts and watch them sizzle, browning them on both sides, then awkwardly cut into the centers to see if they're done. They're still a little pink, but that's fine.

I transfer the breasts to a plate and chop garlic and onions and cook them in the chicken and olive oil fat, then pour in the lentils. I add water and wait until it sinks in. The chicken goes in after that, with sliced tomatoes. Paul is a more precise cook than I am, since he approaches the task with the same scrupulous care as Louis Pasteur took when testing for microorganisms. People, women, are said to enjoy making meals, and I can enjoy it now too, I decide. I close my eyes like I did when I was a child eating Hawaiian Meat. I breathe in the scent of the chicken and listen to the reassuring burble of the lentils. After that, I chop the cilantro and throw the stems and the tomato seeds into the garbage. I see that I did nothing with the kale and put it back in the refrigerator. When twenty minutes have passed, I return to the pan and hover above it, feeling the heat rise to my face.

Where is everybody? Men should be wandering in here saying

nice things about the food. I sprinkle on the cilantro and leave the chicken-lentils on the back burner, realizing that it's three hours until dinnertime. Now that the chicken isn't sizzling, I can hear the faucet dripping again. I'm going to write my report now, I decide, except that I don't. I go into our bedroom. My iPhone sits on my nightstand and I press it to my chest as I lie down on the comforter. I briefly fall asleep and wake back up when I hear Paul speaking to Tomás in a low, tense voice. I can't hear what he's saying. I turn over, push another pillow under my head, and open up Google News.

My screen fills with coverage of the Breonna Taylor protests. Today a Jefferson County grand jury failed to indict Louisville police officers Jonathan Mattingly, Brett Hankison, and Myles Cosgrove, who, last March, burst into the young Black woman's home on the advice of a bad warrant. They shot Breonna Taylor in her chest, abdomen, left forearm, left thigh, and feet. Instead of returning a murder or manslaughter indictment, the grand jury charged Hankison with endangering people who lived in nearby housing. Mattingly and Cosgrove were deemed to have used justifiable force on Taylor, who bled to death on the floor of her apartment at the age of twenty-four.

"The data we obtained is interesting," Somnang says on Zoom. It's September 25. The city lifted the evacuation warnings last night. The sky's a washed-denim blue. It's 81 degrees. I'd thought I'd feel relief when our not dying by wildfire stopped being number one on my to-do list, but new, terrible things always seem to take the place of the last emergency.

I am, again, working from bed. I've put a virtual background of giant, dew-sprinkled blades of grass on my screen. My head and shoulders float within this odd atmosphere, so I look like a fairy or a tiny bug. Somnang shares a screen showing a grainy radar image of a black and white asteroid. Apophis resembles nothing so much as miniature chips of light. But it weighs 26.99 billion kilograms.

"Interesting as in not great," I say.

"No, it's not."

"It looks fine for 2029."

"You know that 2068 is now the problem." Somnang launches into a discussion of evidence that the asteroid is currently drifting off its projected, safe course.

On my computer, Somnang's weathered face seems the same as ever. He doesn't act embarrassed about the things he told me at Goldstone, which makes me glad. For the past two days, Paul and I have worn ourselves out from failing to explain the Breonna Taylor disaster to our son, and I wish I could tell Somnang about that. I think that he would react well to this intimacy, but I don't know how to formulate the immense topic into sentences that are composed of subjects and objects instead of amorphous and sad sounds.

I listen to Somnang as he explains how, given the most recent data, Apophis might crash into the earth in the year Tomás turns sixty-four. When I defend against this scenario with a competing model, he agrees that we must remember what happened in 2004, when new numbers allowed us to call off the alarm on Roy Tucker's big rock, and its Torino level went down to zero. The same thing, he allows, will likely happen again. Still, he says, we have to prepare for the chance that our luck will finally run out—as it did at Tunguska, and as it did for Ann Hodges, and as it did for the dinosaurs during the end of the Cretaceous period. Somnang explains that if Apophis did land here, it wouldn't likely cause the same sort of catastrophe as the kind theorized by Luis Alvarez, the particle physicist and mass murderer who was the first to hypothesize that an asteroid as large as a mountain caused an almost total extinction event over sixty million years ago.

Nevertheless, Somnang tells me, Apophis would do so much

damage that the carnage and destruction of natural resources would be felt for generations. He describes Apophis's composition and postulates on the hundreds of thousands or millions of deaths it would inflict on a populated area if it achieved contact. He describes how the dust its impact would throw up into the sky would affect weather patterns and cause crop demise and drought. He continues talking and talking, about how the meteorite could crack apart not only the earth's crust but also its economy and infrastructure. He mentions the public health problems caused by innumerable unburied corpses. The global geopolitical confusion and its deadly effects. The foreseeable wars over potable water sources and available grains. The volcanism and tsunamis triggered by the great force.

It's time to clean again. I'm in the bathroom, listening to the air conditioner rattle in the hall. I've brought in liquid detergent, Windex, paper towels, a sponge, and a bucket. I open the transom window over the toilet, so that I don't inhale too many chemicals. I'm wearing rubber gloves and a dilapidated Caltech T-shirt and running shorts. I kneel in front of the bathtub and turn on the tap, then put the bucket beneath. I look at the white rush of water. It fills the bucket, spraying my face, which feels good. Turning off the tap, I look into the bucket. My face reflects darkly. The air conditioner thumps and wheezes. Too much time passes with me doing this. I feel like I could get stalled in this moment. I pour the bucket down the drain and put it on the floor next to me. I crawl into the bathtub and sit in it. I stretch out my legs and press my bare feet against the cool wetness at the opposite end of the tub.

After a while, my mother looks in. She observes me with a placid expression, as if my sitting in an empty bathtub while fully dressed isn't original or odd. I see that her hands flower with pink and red splashes of paint. Her hair fluffs around her head like she's been riding in a convertible.

"My chest hurts," I say.

My mother disappears from the doorway. She returns holding a rectangular object in her hand. She closes the bathroom door behind her and sits on the edge of the tub. She opens her fingers and I see she's grasping a box of cigarettes. When she flicks on a lighter, it casts a golden glow on her skin. She lights a cigarette and takes a long drag. I reach out my hand, and she puts the cigarette between my index and middle fingers. For obvious health reasons, I've never smoked in my life, but I fit the cigarette between my lips and draw in. I don't cough. The smoke feels warm and vivid in my throat.

My mother accepts the cigarette when I hand it back, then tucks her hair over her ear. Purple and orange stripes glimmer on the undersides of her forearms. She takes a pull on the cigarette and leans back her head. The smoke shatters upward from her lips, toward the transom window.

Deeper into the afternoon, Mom takes a nap and I go into my bedroom. I close the door and crawl beneath the covers. My eyes close as I lean back, clutching my computer. Between my ribs, I can feel my cells assembling and dissolving, an unsettling sensation that feels like seasickness. The unjoining parts of me move up and down, like concussion waves, and I work hard to glue them back together, using Chinese White I inherited from my mother a long time ago, when I wasn't born yet, but living inside of the black and starry space of her body. . . . The flickers of light that darted through her womb pulse and flare while she runs from Brooks and crosses over the border, but I can hear the light tink of a drop in a bowl. I wrap the Chinese White around it, but it doesn't help. The water comes down.

I open my eyes and sit up, shaking my head. When middle-aged women sleep in the middle of the day it's an Ann Hodges-like sign of depression. Work. I open my computer. Clicking into Chrome, I wade through my files, glancing through my texts on Hodges and Tunguska, academic articles on Apophis, graphs and videos, and upsetting diagnostics of the effects of bomb impacts on populated areas. The accumulated research, which I began collecting at the beginning of the pandemic and now expands to eight gigabytes, flies past me until I settle finally on a black-and-white picture of a man.

Sitting at a table, writing in a notebook, and turning toward the camera in a three-quarter profile, he wears a suit jacket and a smile so stiff it eradicates his upper lip. This is Luis Alvarez, the polymath and killer. The photo was taken when Alvarez taught on the faculty of the University of California, Berkeley, a four-decade long sinecure that supported him whether he devised mass assassination machines in Los Alamos or assembled theories that ranged from the banal and oddball to the stunningly, and world-changingly, brilliant.

A long time ago, something appeared in the sky over the coast of what's now Mexico. Let's say this omega force was black and on fire, like Satan is sometimes depicted in horror movies and in my mother's stories. It sent out terrific booms and blast waves of energy as it streaked into the atmosphere. Long-necked creatures, with wings and bone-crushing jaws and scaly tails, roamed the planet then. These animals looked up when they heard the emergency coming and soon after keeled over, smashing into fern beds and swamps while their eyes rolled wildly in their heads. The swimming life in the ocean died. Almost all vegetation turned black and crumbled away. The world's mammals rolled onto their backs and went rigid. Volcanos spewed orange lava and tsunamis cruised across the sea.

Since first studying Dinosauria fossils in the early 1800s, scientists understood that something swept away these giants, along with most other living things, in one of the worst extinction events ever recorded by the earth's strata. For over a century, thousands of researchers tackled the problem, writing paper upon paper arguing that the cause was climate change, starbursts, magnetic field flips, bacterial infections, or a poisonous accumulation of methane.

Finally, Luis Alvarez solved the mystery of why all the dinosaurs died.

A history of the hazards presented by Near-Earth Objects would be incomplete without an accounting of the Alvarez Hypothesis, which holds that an Everest-sized asteroid crashed on the earth with such force during the Cretaceous–Paleogene era (66 Ma) that approximately 80 percent of all species perished. Except for Moses's biblical descriptions of the meteorite bombardment that destroyed Sodom and Gomorrah, and the Prophet Muhammad's Koranic warning that devils will one day be destroyed by a Blaze, Dr. Luis Alvarez proved one of the first authorities in history to presume that our world could be so destroyed. Before his work, the concept of Earth's liquidation by meteorite or comet seemed beyond human imagining, despite the fact that astrogeologists had been studying the colossal Meteor Crater (Flagstaff, Arizona), the Vredefort Dome (South Africa), and the Sudbury Basin (Ontario, Canada) for many decades by then. General acceptance of the thesis came in 2010, after researchers identified the Chicxulub depression in the Yucatán as the likely location of Alvarez's impact. But when Dr. Alvarez first published the shocking theory in January 1980, it inspired intense, even terrified, reactions.

Why could Dr. Alvarez picture that particular brand of apocalypse while other scientists had overlooked the possibility of an asteroid? In order to solve this puzzle, let us gloss over the rudiments of his biography—the great man's Spanish forebears and 1911 birth in San Francisco; his idyllic California childhood, filled with toys and games; his dazzling feats at University of Chicago's graduate school; his early work with cosmic rays. Instead, we shall leap ahead, all the way to the 1940s, several decades before the curious problems of dinosaurs and minor planets first entered his thoughts. Hunting him down to Hiroshima, Japan, we find Alvarez, a newly minted particle physicist, embroiled in the dark workings of the Manhattan Project.

In 1944 J. Robert Oppenheimer hired Alvarez to reform the design of the Mark III, also known as "Fat Man," whose solid plutonium core could not be compressed fast enough to achieve implosion. Alvarez pursued the solution to this problem with the lavish gifts for logic with which he had been born, quickly devising a high-voltage capacitor that crushed the metal in a flash. Oppenheimer smiled his small smile at the clever device; the Pentagon cheered. Three days before Alvarez's work would annihilate the people of Nagasaki, he achieved the honor of sitting in an observational aircraft that flew in tandem with the B-29 *Enola Gay,* so as to watch the first bombing. The physicists Harold Agnew and Lawrence H. Johnston were the only other scientists in the plane, which had been dubbed with the unlikely moniker *The Great Artiste.* As these geniuses sailed through the sky next to the bomber, Alvarez looked out the window, down at Hiroshima, waiting to see the results of Oppenheimer's vision . . . .

Loud and hot, it was. The roar of engines filled the hull. Alvarez peered down through the tattered clouds and glimpsed the tiny city, which looked like a miniature map made by a fanatical model maker. Agnew and Johnston did the same. The three men did not talk, nor did they look each other in the eye. Next to them, the *Enola Gay* blasted through the azure, a gleaming behemoth holding Little Boy, which the crew had decorated with their signatures.

Alvarez felt sure they should say something, such as, It has to be done, the bomb must be dropped. There is no other way.

He gazed silently at the men in the cabin. Agnew wore the rapt expression of a baseball fan. Johnston's face shone silver as it reflected back the sky. Alvarez turned back to the window.

I didn't set out to do evil, he thought. I only followed my nature.

The *Enola Gay* made a grinding sound. Hatch doors fell open. The aircraft dropped its package.

A pause. No breath. Unreality.

Alvarez saw light, light. Thunder momentarily blotted out his senses. *The Great Artiste* rattled around him like a tin can. White clouds streamed up from below. The pale smoke lifted into the air. It unfolded like a rose.

White smoke soon became black smoke. Gray smoke. Flash of gold. Stream of red.

The thunder ceased. He heard no screams.

Alvarez closed his eyes and rested his forehead against the coolness of the glass.

Days later, he sent his four-year-old son, Walter, a letter.

What regrets I have about being a party to killing and maiming thousands of Japanese civilians this morning are tempered with the hope that this terrible weapon we have created may bring the countries of the world together and prevent further wars. Alfred Nobel thought that his invention of high explosives would have that effect, by making wars too terrible, but unfortunately it had just the opposite reaction. Our new destructive force is so many thousands of times worse that it may realize Nobel's dream.

"Come here and help me, son," I hear Paul call out from the kitchen.

I look up from my screen. From his bedroom, Tomás makes some noncommittal noises I can't decipher.

My fingers rest on my keyboard. I don't know whether I should get up and see what Paul's doing or go back to my work.

But this isn't work anymore, right? I think.

I begin typing again.

Thirty-five years later, after the bombing of Hiroshima and Nagasaki had receded, for some, into remote memory, Luis Alvarez appeared to bear the serenity of a man laureled at Stockholm and protected in his bubble at uc Berkeley. Here, he busied himself with multiple emeritus hobbies, such as searching through the Egyptian pyramids for undiscovered sanctums and subjecting the Zapruder film of John F. Kennedy's assassination to a variety of unpromising optical tests. He was sixty-nine years old, and it seemed as if his best days were behind him.

His son had become a Berkeley geologist. Fixated on a little layer of clay that ran throughout the planet, Walter dashed all over the world, testing samples of the limestone that composed this stratum of the earth that settled after the death of the dinosaurs. Walter's research led him to the Umbrian Apennines, where he dug into the Cretaceous's bleached boundary. Above the seam clustered myriad tiny fossils, and below it scattered giant skeletons. But at this layer of geological history, the crust was blank: No sign of former life would be found. Walter could not begin to divine the cause of the catastrophe. After spending weeks toiling away, he called his father for help. Alvarez leapt onto a plane the next day and shot across the ocean, his heart beating swiftly as he rejoiced over this opportunity to spend time with his child. He arrived in Italy, and with Walter rented a little green Fiat, which they used to speed up and down the region's rose-and-brown hillsides. The two men spent weeks laboring beneath the bright sky as they excavated the layer, studying the white, smooth, empty line running between the thicknesses of bone-rich, pink stone.

Something happened here, Walter said, leaning on his shovel. But what?

Alvarez wiped the sweat from his brow and took a drink from his canteen. He felt unwell, queasy, and thought it might be the heat.

From the articles that you sent me, I see that Simpson believes it was magnetic reversal.

Does that sound right?

Schindewolf says it might have been a supernova.

Is that plausible?

Alvarez stared unseeingly at the green valley below.

Seems like we don't know what to think, he said. Let's go
back to the hotel. Maybe something will come to us.

All right.

Alvarez and Walter packed up their gear and drove their
Fiat down the hillside toward the little pensione they had
rented. It was not much: Alvarez's quarters had a twin bed, a
shabby upholstered chair, a small Frigidaire filled with snacks.
While Walter went off to rest, Alvarez bathed in the bagno
down the hall and then made a shaker of martinis. He wanted
to sleep but couldn't settle down.

He sat in the armchair and finished his drink. His nausea
grew worse. Some ghost of a thought walked through him. He
shivered.

What would cause there to be nothing? he wondered,
clenching his jaw. He saw again the pink stone, then the layer
of white. The little bones above, the great bones below, the
absence between.

What could create all that death?

Suddenly, he saw through it. The revelation came at him
from a dark haze, with bright flashes. The room grew strangely
silent and then seemed to disappear. What was this place? It
was the old memory, or perhaps he was asleep and it was a
dream? Something came down from the white sky. The pale,
quiet world had lain far below *The Great Artiste*. Next to their
plane, the *Enola Gay* barreled forward through the azure.
Agnew looked enraptured. Johnston's face reflected the silver
of the sky. No, no, *this* extinction did not occur during the war,
it happened long ago, when prodigious creatures roamed.
Yet, he understood that its cause was somehow similar to the
bomb. But this object was large, like Everest, or the Matterhorn.
It burst into flames. It shone, metallic, and was inscribed with
God's name.

The Thing followed its nature. It plummeted toward the

earth. The young globe shone greenly, nestled in tattered rags
of mist. The mountain hit the ground. Light, light. Then, white
steam? Yes, and dark smoke, rising. Black smoke, gray smoke.
Flash of gold. Stream of orange. The ground became fire.

If it was a meteorite, he knew, groaning, they should test for
iridium. And also platinum. Osmium. Rhodium.

Alvarez closed his eyes, remembering the letter he sent
Walter in the days after he watched Hiroshima go up in flames.

Sometimes you can't believe the things that you've done,
he wanted to tell his boy now.

But he could not move from the room, nor even speak, for
a long time.

I close my EliteBook. The painted ceiling above me is bright
white, though it's crazed with little cracks and small stains. The
quilt spreads out over my legs. It has a wedding ring pattern,
made up of white and blue squares and sprinkled with tiny tulips.
Paul and I bought it in the 1990s at a yard sale because I thought
it looked old-fashioned and romantic. My hands run across the
colors as I listen to my computer whirr.

No, I've lost the thread, I think, throwing back the covers.
Whatever I'm doing isn't connected to my job anymore. It's something else.

After Alvarez did his bit to help Truman win the war, he
aimed his lipless grin at a wall of flashing cameras when he won
the 1968 Nobel Prize for his early discoveries in particle physics. It was only in that swinging decade that he began to show
an obsession with death that would launch him from being a
mere Nobelist to enjoying the rare status that he retains today.
He fixated on the Zapruder movie and labored unsuccessfully
to prove that the backward snap of Kennedy's head meant the
president had been shot from behind, and so never saw the thing
that killed him. After that, Alvarez decamped for Egypt, where

he sent cosmic rays through the pyramids of Giza in the dashed hopes of finding hidden burial chambers, so he could recover the bodies of the unnamed dead. The Alvarez hypothesis would prove his last, most perfect, and greatest expression of guilt over Hiroshima and Nagasaki.

In 1988 Alvarez died in the bed of a Berkeley hospital, surrounded by family and doctors. Beyond that one, anodyne letter sent to Walter after Hiroshima, there isn't anywhere, in all the records, a single sign that, after August 1945, he wondered if he should never have been born. The only evidence suggesting that his memory of the bomb damaged his conscience beyond repair is the way he lurched toward the mysteries of destruction during the last decades of his life. Alvarez isn't the one who determined that the dinosaurs were obliterated by an asteroid that landed at Chicxulub, Mexico, my mother's hometown, but he and Walter were the first scientists to theorize about what the fishers of my mother's community had known for generations, maybe centuries, and taught each other through their stories. In a way, Luis Alvarez is, for me, a bridge between science and Brother Death, I think. But I don't know what to do with this information.

Does it matter anyway? I shake off my fantasy of Alvarez suffering in his Umbrian pensione, rubbing my face as I get out of bed. From the TV room come the recorded sounds of female squabbling, and a knocking issues from the kitchen. I head toward Tomás's room. My son wouldn't speak much last night, while Paul and I Googled how the grand jury functions and tried to explain how what happened in the Breonna Taylor case was technically legal but wrong, wrong, wrong. Tomás replied that he wanted to be with Cecil, that he wanted to talk to Cecil, that only Cecil would know how he felt. He'd sat at the kitchen table with his fists on his knees and his mouth tightened in that strange way again. "You don't understand," he kept saying, while Paul and I sent desperate coded messages to each other with our eyes and our hands. When I go to his room now, I see that it's empty. Also, the calculus book remains in the same place on his nightstand. I sit down on his bed, smoothing the covers with my hands. The knocking sounds, metal upon metal, are getting louder. I move toward the kitchen.

Tomás is lying on the floor with his head and shoulders under the sink. Paul crouches next to him, peering under. They've removed the tape that I wound around the leaking pipe and thrown it aside. A red aluminum box, covered with dust and exhumed from the garage, sits in the middle of the room, and rejected tools scatter here and there.

"Like this?" Tomás asks, his elbow moving.

"Looks right," Paul says.

"It's just a little . . . sticky."

"It's old, we should probably get it replaced."

"I think I got it."

"Good, good."

"Can you give me the other thing?"

Paul stands up and goes to the toolbox, where he rummages in a clanking mess of metal. He sees me standing in the doorway and makes a kissing mouth, then hands a wrench to Tomás.

"Screw it in," he says.

"Okay." Tomás's elbow moves up and down. "I think this'll do it."

Paul puts the tools back in the box. I grab some paper towels from the counter and mop up puddles that have oozed out onto the floor.

"The paper you asked me to read, I'll look at it tonight," I say to my husband.

He has dust in his hair. A smear of grease dots his right cheek. Still squatting by the toolbox, he looks at me over his shoulder and his cheek dimples.

"I love you," he sings.

5
The Late Heavy Bombardment

It has been assumed widely that most melt bodies resulting from ancient impacts have disappeared on account of erosion. The presence of a typical mafic, such as basalt, does not confirm, in the contemporary scientific imagination, a prior meteorite contact. The rejection of basalts as a signature of meteorite collisions stems from the rocks' prominence in the earth's crust and their manufacture during volcanism. We suspect, additionally, that the widespread presence of basaltic boulders, stones, and pebbles in the modern landscape disqualifies them from recognition as hallmarks of impact events. Present-day superstitions, enriched by a modern ignorance of the ubiquity of traumatic happenings, presume cataclysmic meteorite arrivals to be unique occurrences.

That one may not wander among the dells of the Sudbury Basin without tripping upon basaltic outcroppings fails to spark the faintest noesis within the larger community of planetary scientists, despite the fact that it is a well-known impact site. That a person might stumble upon a vast panorama of flood basalt at ground zero in the Loran Lake also does not inspire enlightenment amongst our benighted peers. In this paper, however, we prove that in the Vredefort Dome, basaltic elements *created by* the Vredefort impact (2023 ± 4

Ma; Paleoproterozoic) may be seen sprinkled far and wide across the
site's flower-fringed half circle of hills. We rely upon an innovative use
of Wasserburg's methodology for dating, as well as analysis of geo-
chemical anomalies, in making our case. In presenting this research,
we write with the hope that our elucidation of the obvious may take
an axe to the frozen sea of misconception that plagues our profession.

W ell, your dad isn't afraid of making people angry," I say
to Tomás, while Paul bashes his forefingers into his keyboard. It's the next morning, September 26. In fifteen minutes,
I have to go to a doctor's appointment, and I'm standing in the
doorway of my husband's office with a purse hanging off my
shoulder and a draft of his paper in my hands. On the other side
of the room, Tomás sits at my desk and reads *The Plague* as if he
comes in here all the time to hang out with his father. Which he
doesn't. I don't think I've seen him come into this room since he
met Cecil. It must be some leftover good feeling from the father/
son plumbing adventure yesterday.

"He gets that bad attitude from me," Tomás jokes.

"What did you think?" Paul asks, not looking my way.

I flick through the pages with my thumb. "That it'll make
waves, like you always do."

Paul peers at the ceiling. "What I want is for people to believe me."

"You could work on your tone."

Paul rolls his chair away from his desk and turns so he faces
the office window, which looks out over the backyard. "Probably."

"Maybe that's why you're getting so many rejections from
journals," Tomás says.

"How did you know I was getting rejections?"

"Because you talk about it to Mom in a really loud voice, ba-
sically all the time."

Following Paul's hooded gaze, I see the lawn chairs that

remain positioned in socially distanced antipodes from back when we had Cecil and Blessica over for lunch.

"They're just not interested in my idea," he says.

I hand him back his paper, which I've lightly copyedited. "I like it."

Paul glowers at the pencil marks and checks I've written in his manuscript's margins. After a couple minutes, he puts down the small stack and stands from his chair, jingling the change in his pockets.

"Okay, let me get my wallet. We'll take you."

"No, no," I say. "You're not coming. It's just an annual."

"Mom, where are you going?"

"To the doctor."

"It's not one of those scans?" Paul asks.

"I won't need someone to drive me home, so they won't let you in."

"We can come anyway," Paul says. "Wait in the car outside."

"It's nothing, I don't need you to go. You two stay here and have fun."

Tomás turns a page of his book. "Have fun doing what?"

"You could fix some more of the house."

"No," Paul says.

"No," Tomás says, at the same time.

I straighten the photographs that stand in formation on Paul's desk. "It was good, you guys fixing the sink."

"Sometimes a person just needs to work with their hands." Paul grins. "But not too much."

"Maybe you two should do more of that kind of thing," I say. "Play ball, or . . . board games? Get a hobby, like woodworking."

"Darling, stop worrying."

"Yeah, Mom, we're okay."

"You look at your phone too much," I say to my son. "And you're not doing your homework. You're not doing the problems

I give you. You're playing video games. Sliding behind. And I've been reading the studies about COVID and learning outcomes. What if you can't come back from it?"

"Mom, come on."

"Laura," Paul says softly, "he'll snap back."

"How do you know?"

"I went through a bit of this myself when I was young," my husband tells me.

"No, when you were his age. . . ." I almost say, *You were a math prodigy; you were a genius,* but I manage to stop myself, so that Tomás isn't hurt by the comparison. "When you were young, you were fine."

"That's not entirely true. There was a period when I ran into difficulty. I stopped—well, most things."

"'Most things?'" I repeat.

Tomás furrows his brow. "Dad, what do you mean?"

"When my father . . ." Paul hesitates.

"Was murdered by the cops," Tomás says too bluntly.

Paul closes his eyes. "When that happened, I didn't do much of anything but walk miles and miles and then sit at the dome, looking out at the grass."

I nod. "You told me that when we first met."

Paul remains quiet, until I realize that something is happening. I watch him and wait.

"What I didn't tell you is that, after he passed, I stopped going to school for a while," he says. "I stopped reading. I stopped talking. I stopped eating. I had to be hospitalized." He clears his throat and gives Tomás and me a shy smile. "And, in the end, I was perfectly all right."

"Hospitalized for what?" Tomás asks.

"I was upset."

"I don't understand, 'upset?'" I ask.

"Just that. Upset."

"You weren't 'upset,'" I say. "Babe, your father *died.*"

"Yes."

"I'm 'upset,'" I say. "The mailman's 'upset.' The checkout lady at Trader Joe's 'upset.' Everybody's 'upset.' 'Upset' doesn't get you hospitalized."

"Fine. I . . . I thought I knew things other people didn't."

Tomás puts down his book. "Things like what?"

Paul doesn't answer.

My son and I look at each other.

"Dad," Tomás says, "were you suicidal?"

Paul smiles at us again in a gentle, sorry way. Tomás's face twinges with emotion. Paul walks around his desk and embraces me. I look down, at the photograph of his father, Jabulani, in its silver frame. After Pasadena lifted the evacuation warning, I'd carefully removed it and its siblings from the duffel bag and placed them in their original location, just to the left of the blotter where Paul handwrites his first drafts.

"No, no, no, no, no, of course not," Paul says, in a tone that I can't read.

At 8:45 I'm in the Volvo, driving to Burbank. Cars jerk and pivot at intersections. A horn yells at me as I mistime a left-hand turn. The vehicles thicken into a glittering barricade on the 134 so that my speed slows to thirty MPH. The traffic is bad again, unlike in March and April when the freeways stood vacant. I squint into the sun cutting through my windshield and can't find my sunglasses in my purse, which disgorges all my garbage on the seat next to me. I'm having trouble concentrating on the freeway's many moving parts because I can't focus; my mind jams with question marks and barking noise. I'm not quite sure what my husband just told my son and me.

The exit is Buena Vista. I pay at the machine in the lot and park, then take a few minutes to find my mask and get it on and put everything back into my bag. I have two scans today because I put off my medical appointments in 2019 and then was too scared to go in the spring. Entering the hospital, I check in with the guard, who takes my temperature and makes me put on a fresh mask and also gloves. I grab another mask just to be safe and strap that one on too. The foyer is large, falsely marble, beige, and cold. At the far left side is a sofa where a nurse or a nurse's attendant lies down, maskless and staring at her phone.

Up on the third floor I take a chair in the small waiting room, which is decorated with ersatz Victorian prints showing white ladies holding parasols while being rowed down the River Cam. A woman sits five chairs down from me. She's elderly, with colorless hair and delicate, eroded hands. Soon a female nurse wearing a mask, a plastic shield, gloves, booties, and a plastic bag-like jacket comes and takes her away. On papers I've been given, I write down my name, weight, age, address, ethnicity, family history, and run my pen through the line of NO boxes attached to questions regarding previous personal experiences with diseases like cancer and cardiac arrest.

The nurse wearing all the plastic comes back. She brings me into a changing room, where I take off my T-shirt and change into a pale-blue cotton gown printed with pink roses. I put my clothes in a locker that has a little black key with a curly rubber handle sticking out of it. I slip the key wristlet on and stand out in the hall. The nurse reappears and leads me to a small room, which hosts a female technician, who also looks laminated in her PPE. At the center of the room is an upholstered table overtopped by a large, white metal contraption with a long arm. A computer with a monitor occupies the southwest corner of the room. The air smells of rubbing alcohol and citrus.

The technician and I exchange greetings and casually offer each other our impressions of shock and horror at the pandemic and the presidency. She gestures at me to lie down on the table and I do so. Moving back to the computer, she tells me to stay still and the machine moves its arm over my hips and lower back. This goes on for a few minutes, after which she brings me back out to the waiting area. Soon the nurse shows up again and leads me to the elevator.

We go to the fourth floor, and I enter a large white room that hosts a male technician. A huge white metal donut with a slide-out bed sticking out of its hole presides here like a futuristic altar. The technician is my age and Latino. He has gray hair on his temples and nice eyes above his mask. He tells me to put the key wristlet down on a chair that stands by the door. I do that, then open the front of my gown and lie on the bed coming out of the metal donut, stomach down. He says that the scan will be with contrast and without contrast. From his pocket, he brings out orange earplugs and tucks them into my ears while I hold my head up in an effort to help him.

The bed is like a massage table in that it has a hole for the face, but it also has two other holes that I fit my breasts into. I stick my face into the face hole and try to breathe through my two masks while stretching my arms and hands above my head. The man leaves the room and I close my eyes and the bed rolls into the middle of the donut. From here commences a series of sounds like gunshots, interspersed with a recorded and weirdly sooth-ing woman's voice that commands me to stop breathing and then to breathe. The man occasionally speaks to me from an unseen speaker and asks me if I'm having any problems, like claustro-phobia. I say no. Eventually the gunshots stop, and for a while I lie there with my arms raised as if I'm being arrested. Finally, the bed moves out of the donut, and the man reappears, wheel-ing an IV beside him. He sticks a needle into my arm and tapes it tightly in place. I taste metal and feel warmth spread from my throat down to my vagina. The man leaves and the bed goes in and the gunshots sound again and the female Hal voice tells me to breathe and not to breathe. I close my eyes and think of Paul.

After what seems like a long, long time, the man comes back and takes the IV out of my arm and says that I did a good job. He helps me up off the table and extracts my earplugs and puts the key wristlet on me, and walks me out of the room and back down the hall. Here, I'm met again by the nurse, who tells me to come with her. She leads me to another room, and I sit on its exam table. She asks me to wait.

"But I thought that I could just go home after?" I ask.

"The radiologist said that he wanted you to just stay for a minute."

"Why?"

"Sometimes they want people to stay a little longer."

"Why?"

"He'll tell you everything when he comes in."

"Could he have seen the images already? We just did the scan. Did he see something bad?"

She refuses to answer and leaves. I wait in my little robe. This room has a watercolor of flowers hanging on the wall and a chest with medical supplies in it and some posters that announce things about patients' rights. The space is painted gray-blue. I stare at an empty spot on the wall and think about Paul some more. I can feel my heart rate gaining speed within me, it feels like a physical pressure, a kind of gas or a fire rising up inside of my chest and my throat. Another interminable period goes by and then the nurse, not a male radiologist, comes back. She says that the doctor wants a couple more images. I say nothing but just stand up, and she leads me back to the room with the donut. The same male technician is there and he says that this one can be without contrast. I get on the sliding bed-thing again and he puts in the earplugs and the table goes into the donut.

The gunshots start again. I'm eating my masks with the effort to breathe. I'm stripped of all sensation by the time the scan ends.

The nurse has returned and touches me on the arm, then she takes me back to the room with the flower watercolor. I sit, sweating, on the exam table and look at the empty spot on the wall again. I tell myself how this is fine, this is actually helpful, in a sick way, because, when you think about it, many of the asteroid researchers who made important discoveries about potentially hazardous objects had first gone through hell, a way worse hell than this. Their going through hell had helped them be almost insanely alert to unfathomable dangers, which turned out to be a great thing for space science. There had been Leonid Kulik going through hell during the Russo-Japanese War, and that let him understand what had happened at Tunguska. Luis Alvarez went through hell, too, because he was a mass murderer, and that helped him solve how all the dinosaurs died. Gerald Wasserburg, another astronomy hero, also went through a supremely bad hell, during World War II, and it helped him figure out how asteroids once destroyed and remade our solar system. I have a suspicion, too, that Roy Tucker might have also gone through hell during the Vietnam War, which is why he was able to find Apophis.

All those great, great men made asteroid history because they'd gone through terrible pain, and that lesson allowed them to see what other people couldn't. And now there's me, too, the me who is here in this gray-blue room, waiting to hear about whether the donut says I have a problem. And I'm also waiting to see if my family is going to die of COVID or cancer or wildfires or from getting shot by a police officer. And then I guess there's the additional fact that Paul apparently had some mental health issues I've never heard about before and that are hopefully not genetic. But at least I can tell myself that this, my own personal hell, could maybe someday help me make an amazing discovery, like Kulik and Alvarez and so on. Except, I think, remembering the picture of Ann Hodges and her big bruise, this fear is only going to help me if I can somehow see through it. I need to *see through it,* all the way to the other side, assuming, that is, that there *is* something beyond this, and not just more death and horribleness and total terror.

As I'm mentally ranting all of this a white man wearing a mask and a kind of plastic suit and rubber gloves and booties enters the room carrying my file. Then all my ideas disappear, and I'm emptied of every emotion except for frozen blankness.

"Okay," he says.

"Hi," I say.

"Okay," he repeats, reading my file, "Laura. Everything looks good since that last biopsy, which was fine."

"Okay," I say.

"I mean, the breasts look good."

I don't ask about why he had to take another MRI or X-ray or whatever it is, I just want to get out of there.

"Great," I say.

"Your bones, though."

I look at him.

"Some osteopenia."

I do not say anything.

"That's the precursor to osteoporosis."

"I know."

"We don't have another bone scan in your file."

"I got busy."

"Is there a family history?"

"Yes."

"Your numbers are actually on the edge of osteoporosis."

"Oh."

"There are medicines," he says. "Phosphates."

"Yes." My mother hated those pills, she said they were killing her, and so she stopped taking them and that is why her bones are crumbling and vanishing.

"You can talk about it with your gynecologist," he says. "Or go to a specialist."

I'm shaking, but not so hard that he can see. "Can my son get it?"

"Your son?"

"Can my son inherit it?"

"I'd ask the specialist about things like that."

"Thank you, doctor."

The radiologist tells me to take care and exits the room, his PPE making noises like Saran Wrap being peeled away from a submarine sandwich. The nurse comes back and leads me to the changing room. I slip out of the cotton robe and open the locker with the key. I pull on my T-shirt and get my purse. I am nauseated. I leave the key in the locker and exit the building.

An hour later, I'm at home, in the living room. When I'd first arrived back from the hospital, I forced myself to look normal as I checked in on my family. I'd reassured them that my tests all went fine and then gone to bed with my computer. Upon lying down among the covers in the middle of the sunshiny day, I started shaking again and suddenly felt the claustrophobia the medical technician had asked me about when I was in the donut. Deciding that sitting upright on a sofa is better for modeling resilience, I made my way to this deserted part of our house. I now plug my computer into the wall socket and put it on the sofa seat. Moving the pink throw pillow, I plant myself on the cushion next to the armrest. My computer tilts back and forth on my lap. The pillow fits nicely on my thighs and I balance the computer on that.

Three clicks on my keyboard and I'm back in my *History of Hazardous Objects* dossier. I scoot past a dozen files and open one titled "Gerald Wasserburg." It contains texts and clips about the eminent geologist, the one who'd gone through hell like Kulik and Alvarez and Tucker and whom I'd been thinking about in the breast clinic. In 1974 Gerald Wasserburg changed the future of planetary science when he first published a theory that painted ancient space as a site of clashing titans and exploding stars. I review an account of Wasserburg's early, and disturbing, military career before skimming a few of his famous studies and some video recreations of his famous hypothesis. Soon my computer screen sparkles with an artist's animated rendering of flaming asteroids smashing fiery pits into Earth, Saturn, and the Moon. After seeing Earth get destroyed several times, I open my Word file and tap out:

> This report's brief review of NEOS must also contend with the most sustained incidence of impact events in our solar system's history, which would be the Late Heavy Bombardment (4.1–1.8 Ga). As Dr. G. Wasserburg reported in the 1970s, Mercury, Venus, Earth, the Moon, and Mars faced an existential threat

I stop typing. I'm no longer shaking, but I feel Gerald Wasserburg float away from me like an astronaut ejected from his pod, his arms reaching out and his legs kicking through space. I breathe into my palms, studying the stripes of white screen glare and black type that I can see through my fingers. The sound of MRI gunshots replays in my mind like an old and catchy song. Finally, my email *pings*. My tech automatism kicks in, and I toggle from Wasserburg to Outlook. My inbox contains an invitation to a protest, which will take place downtown tomorrow night. The emails seem to self-generate, and I read about a food bank that's about to go bankrupt, a fund for newly homeless restaurant workers, and a bail fund. I donate to each with PayPal and soon find myself looking at CNN.

Beneath the site's red-and-white banner, I see a picture of

a Black woman yelling into a megaphone. Next to her stands a Black man wearing a mask that says *Breonna Taylor.* Under the photo I read that, last night, a car crashed through an action in Yorba Linda, California, and hit two people. In Portland, Oregon, police shot protesters with "pepper balls," which I know are breakable bullets made out of corrosives. In Seattle, there have been marches and reports of "standoffs." Police discharged projectiles into these crowds too. I have to look up the term "blast balls" and learn that these are nonlethal grenades that fragment into shrapnel, which can pierce the head and the face.

I pick up my phone, press the icon of the bleeding heart, and put my fingers over the light: 91. My chest expands and contracts. In my mind, I can see pepper and blast balls flying through the firelit air and exploding on teenagers. Some time passes, wherein I begin to feel confused, and eventually this image blurs and reforms into a clear picture of asteroids flinging themselves through space. Apparently, I focus on this hallucination for some length of time, doing and seeing and hearing nothing as if euthanized until I realize that my mother is talking to me.

"Laura," she says.

I look up. Mom bears down on me, her face framed by her hair, which curves into points like two silver scimitars. Her hands rest on her hips.

"Time to get some fresh air."

"Mom, I will, in just a minute."

"Let's go, you need to get outside."

My mother removes my computer from my lap, grasps my hand, and leads me through the living room while favoring her left leg. We move through the hallway, the kitchen, and out the back door. She puts me in one of the chairs that maybe will remain here as a permanent reminder of the crying-picnic and lowers herself gingerly into its companion. I see that she's bending her body to keep her left sit-bone from touching the metal seat, so I run back into the house and get the pink pillow from the living room sofa. After coming back outside, I put the pillow under her bottom and she sits on it, nodding. Together, we look out at the yard, with its brown grass and wilting weeds.

"We'll just rest in the sun here," my mother says, closing her eyes. "It's good for the soul."

"I read something about COVID and Vitamin D."

"We're not going to talk about COVID."

"Also, Vitamin D is good for your bones."

"Not talking about that either."

"Okay."

"We're just going to relax," she says.

"All right."

My mother and I stay silent for a little while the sun pours down.

"I'm messed up," I say.

"I know."

"I mean, I think that I am just completely fucked up right now."

"Just breathe," my mother says.

"That's what my gynecologist said."

"Smart lady."

"She had some breathing exercise that she wanted me to do but I can't remember it now."

"Doesn't got to be anything fancy."

I close my eyes and feel the sunrays generate a small hot flash somewhere around my collarbones. I open one eye and see my mother meditating. She raises her face to the sky and smiles, turning up the blue, paint-splashed palms of her hands so they cup the day's sunshine as if it were water.

"You know," she says. "The garden could use some help."

"The garden?"

"Nice if you had some more plants around here."

"Oh, okay, yeah."

She opens her eyes and we both look at the yard.

"I don't really have time," I say, my voice cracking. "I'm already so behind on this report."

"Maybe some daisies there," she says. "And some lavender there."

"Lavender."

"Maybe some poppies."

I blink at the grass, trying to get into the spirit. "Roses, I guess, maybe?"

"No."

"Okay." I rack my mind for species of plant life. "Cacti. They're easy, I think."

Mom gesticulates like a symphony conductor, dragging me out of myself with talk about colors, textures, and scents. Lavender, she tells me, is a good choice because it attracts butterflies. I should think about a small herb garden, on the southern edge, with thyme and marjoram, so that I can pick some when making dinner. And maybe cactuses, but also a big aloe—they're a great idea because they never die and you can put their gel on the skin when there are burns or paper cuts.

Two hours later, I've spent way more money than I planned at Home Depot and am thrusting my hands wrist-deep into the earth. Crates of potted plants line up in rows by the back fence. Paul and Tomás have carried out one of the upholstered chairs from the living room and placed it next to the southernmost side of the backyard where I work. My mother sits in the chair, directing my efforts while sipping a Diet Coke and smoking a cigarette.

"You have to really dive into it," she says. "Get some dirt under your nails."

I finger the lavender plants. "Why does this feel so good?"

"Just does. Don't worry about it."

"Lavender here?"

"And beside that, the poppies. Purple and orange together are wow."

"Okay."

Once I've torn up the weeds and loosened the ground with my fingers and a spade, I add a layer of new dirt, which spills out of its bag like cookie crumbs. I turn on the hose. A cold spray soaks the soil. Scent wafts up and mingles with the heat, reminding me of the perfume of a forest floor and also something I can't name. The lavender plants, with their furry, dusky flowers, drop out of their plastic holders when I turn them upside down. I dig holes and tuck them in, sculpting the dirt around the roots. I put my thumb on the hose's mouth and watch it shed a rainbow over the raised bed. Birds cheep and trill from nearby trees.

"So," my mother says.

"Am I watering too much?"

"Probably. It's normal. Gardening can be exciting."

I turn off the hose and begin weeding the next section of the yard.

"So," my mother says. "Once there was a Witch-Queen."

I'm laughing. "Mom. No more stories."

"Once there was a Witch-Queen, and she was the most beautiful and powerful woman in the world."

I yank out all the weeds and rake and pour on some more of the good new dirt.

"The Witch-Queen ruled her kingdom like a lioness," my mother goes on. "She'd sit on her throne with her crown glittering with pearls and her silver hair flowing down her shoulders like the smoke of a great fire. She lorded over a land full of rivers and forests and mountains and lakes. And she wouldn't take shit from anybody.

"The Witch-Queen had two special powers: the power to throw lightning bolts and the power to make rain. With these gifts, she made big wars against her enemy, a crazy country called Gringolandia. She'd hop on top of her magic flying crocodile and scream, 'Off with their heads!' while her girl soldiers waved their light sabers in salute. You see, because there were no men in their whole country, only Amazons who were trained in the ancient art of kung fu.

"Oh, you should have seen the Witch-Queen on her crocodile, which had a tongue made of fire. The crocodile would crawl out of its forest cave and gaze at the Witch-Queen with its big eyes, which shone at her like two stars. It would nuzzle up to her like a poodle and bring her dead toads and gold treasure as gifts. And when she climbed on its back and said, 'Hey, crocodile, let's go!' the beast would give out a roar and fly over Gringolandia.

"The Witch-Queen had the best time! Up there in the sky, hanging on to her crocodile's scales, she'd cackle until the lightning came down on her enemies and zapped them into smoking black cinders. She'd sing a secret song, and the rain would pour down and drown them in their beds. Then she'd give the sign, and her lady warriors would go running in and pillage everything in sight. And the Witch-Queen was happy."

I'm tugging the poppies out of their plastic containers and gently tucking them into the dirt.

"Then one day a strange thing happened, which is that a gringo somehow breached the defenses of the kingdom. Because the Witch-Queen's domain had a lot of security, not only the Amazons with their light sabers and the crocodile, but also grizzly bears that could tear you apart with one swipe of their claws and an army of killer robots. Nobody knew how this big, tall gabacho, handsome, a little older, and with a big thing, had slipped in without all the alarms going off.

"But there the guy was, standing in front of the Witch-Queen, who sat on her throne, and he was wearing a lot of hair oil and a liar's smile and a little speedo so that she could see what was what. He'd brought her one perfect red rose that he kept hidden behind his back. The Amazon warriors jumped to their feet, ready to protect their Queen to the death. And they screamed and began whipping their light sabers in the air like samurais when he offered his rose to the Queen.

"Well, the Witch-Queen looked down at this man, and do you know what she did? She thought: 'He is cute.' If you know anything, then you know 'he is cute' are the three most dangerous words that a woman can ever allow in her mind! She bent down and took the rose from the gringo, and when she looked into his eyes, the most awful thing in the world happened, which is that she fell in love."

I'm placing the poppies right by the lavender and cannot believe that purple next to orange is such a stunning combination. The sun is shining in my eyes, sweat is pouring down my neck, and my hands feel fantastic deep in the warm earth.

"Okay, so now they were in love and they started making sex like crazies. The Amazon girls were like, 'What the fuck is the Witch-Queen doing with this güero when she should be screaming, "off with his head!" and leading us into battle? Meanwhile, the Witch-Queen was too busy bumping butts with the gringo to even notice that nobody was feeding her crocodile, who was wasting away in his cave so that his bones turned into dust and he got depressed. The sex the gringo gave her was so good that she went totally bananas and became like his slave.

"So he had it good. But was it good enough for the gringo? No. One day, he realized that he didn't like that the Witch-Queen was a supreme ruler while he was just a stupid gabacho. So he yelled at her that he was THE MAN and hit her across the mouth so that she tasted blood, and he punched her in the stomach. Finally, she couldn't take it anymore and cackled so that lightning would come down from the sky and kill him dead. But nothing happened. Then she sang her magic song so that the storms would come down and drown the gringo, but not a cloud appeared in the heavens. And she realized that he had stolen her powers with his Thing.

"Now the Witch-Queen was scared. Calling for her crocodile, she raced past the dead bears, and she tripped over the broken robots, until she finally reached the forest cave. And when she got there, the poor crocodile was barely alive; it was so thin, so weak; it was starving to death; it'd been abandoned for too long. When it saw her come in, it tried to smile, but it could only make the tiniest spark between its teeth."

I still have my hands in the wet earth but stop gardening and just listen.

"The Witch-Queen said, 'Oh, oh, oh, oh, my beautiful crocodile, what have I done?'

"And the crocodile said, 'Don't worry about it, everybody makes mistakes.'

"The Witch-Queen embraced the crocodile, who looked at her with his big, sad eyes, and she wept. She said, 'Crocodile, never will I have a friend in my life as good as you, and so you and I will die here together.'

"The crocodile looked at her with his fading eyes and said, 'My Witch-Queen, you must live. You're going to have a baby.'

"And the Witch-Queen knew that the crocodile was right because she hadn't had her period in six weeks. She cried into its neck, 'I don't care, I made a mistake, and now I will never leave you.'

"The crocodile said no. 'That asshole you made sex with now wants you dead, and so you got to flee, so you can protect your child.'

"'Don't leave me!' she cried. She kissed the crocodile's big nose and hugged him tight around its neck. 'Please, I will do anything, don't go.'

"The crocodile looked at her one last time with its eyes, which were like a candle being blown out by the wind. Only the smallest ember could be seen between its jaws.

"At that moment, the Witch-Queen knew such grief, she thought her heart would break.

"'I love you,' the poor beast said. And then it died."

I am crying with my hands still stuck in the earth. My back hunches as I let out long, silent sobs. The tears drip from my face onto the poppy petals and into the dirt. My chest feels like it's going to split. My ribs hurt. My cheeks turn hot, and my mouth is open, and no sound is coming out.

My mother stays in her seat and says, "It's okay."

My body shudders. My throat chokes. A long line of spit drops from my lower lip and falls onto the ground. My fingers clench the dirt. My head is throbbing.

"Just cry, just cry," she says.

I lie down on the grass, resting my face on my forearms, feeling the dirt on my cheek. I sob, jerking, until I feel something release from me, and the rhythm begins to slow.

"You're all right," my mother tells me.

The last weeping leaves me. I lie there for a minute, breathing. It takes some time before I can hear the birds again and feel the sun on my skin. I sit up, dazed, staring at the flowers.

"Let's go inside," she says.

I press my hands on my eyes. "I haven't planted everything."

"We'll do it later."

I wipe my hands on my jeans and help my mom up and we go inside the house. We enter the kitchen and I sit down at the table. My mother gets the kettle from the stove and fills it with water. As it boils, she waddles to the freezer, pulls out the ice cream, and puts it on the counter. She gets some bowls from the cupboard and spoons from the drawer. From another cupboard, she gets the bag of Milanos. She scoops out ice cream into four bowls and sticks in Milanos and spoons. She makes some herbal tea in a pot and covers it with a knitted cozy and gets down four ceramic mugs from a shelf.

Tomás now comes in, holding papers and a pen. He looks at us, then sits down at the table next to me, not mentioning my blotchy face or the fact that I'm stained with dirt. He puts his papers and pen down on the table, and I see that he's done his calculus problems. My mother hands me some paper towels, which she's wetted under the tap. I wipe my face and take up Tomás's math pages while Mom gives him a bowl of ice cream and a cup of tea.

Mom and Tomás talk quietly about the protests as they eat their ice cream and I correct the calculus. Mom takes my paper towels and throws them away. When I'm finished, I tell Tomás that he missed #6 and #15, but the rest are good. Mom gives me my bowl of ice cream and I eat it.

"Let's go into the TV room," she says, when I finish.

In the den, Mom's art supplies are strewn everywhere: watercolor sets and felt-tip pens and watercolor pens and graphite pencils and colored pencils, mugs full of colored water and brushes, and big and small pads of paper. Mom tells Tomás and me to sit on the sofa and gives us pads of paper and felt-tip pens. She sits in her chintz chair with a big pad that is already full of drawings and flips through the pages. She dips a brush into a jar of darkened rinse water, swooshes it onto a cake of color, and paints a bunch of gray-black loops onto a fresh sheet.

I begin drawing orbits with my pen and Tomás draws a wild tangle of crazy lines.

After a while Mom says, "Show me."

We both show her our pads.

"You have to relax your wrist," she says.

I move the pen around and around. "I'm just making some orbits."

"Like this, like this," she says, flicking her hand in the air. "Like a dance."

I draw a loop on a piece of paper.

"There we go," she says. "Beautiful."

"I'm making something for Cecil," Tomás says.

"Like a valentine," Mom says.

"Right." Tomás draws a heart on his pad. "I can give it to him tomorrow."

"Tomorrow when?" I ask.

"There's a protest."

I draw another loop. I don't mention what happened in Portland or Seattle. I don't discuss blast balls or pepper balls. I already know that we're going to the protest because of what happened to Breonna Taylor. Also, I'm depleted, as if I've been wrung out by two huge hands. I haven't cried that way since I was a small child.

"What's an orbit, again?" Tomás asks, after a few minutes.

"There's a theory that we could detect NEOs by sending earth-returning satellites into space," I say. "Their routes would be based on a previous mission called CONTOUR, which failed, but was launched in order to study a couple of comets back in 2002 . . ."

I stop talking when I realize they're not listening to me.

"They're roses," my mother says, "like the roses I used to draw."

"They do look like roses," Tomás says.

"She was always good at drawing, she got it from me," Mom says.

"Okay," I say.

"Like that?" Tomás asks, showing us a big swirly abstract shape.

"Yes, that's excellent," Mom says.

"Yes, it's very nice," I say.

"You need to learn how to draw first, before you can graduate to watercolor," Mom says.

My mother, son, and I stop talking. The flap of paper and the scratchings of felt tips add their music to our silence. My mother finishes her drawing and opens up a watercolor set. She washes the page with brilliant shades of cerulean and sap green and orange. Her brush looks like a magic wand. She tosses her hair theatrically as she works. Tomás settles back into the sofa, drawing huge rhombuses and spirals on page after page. His face concentrates in a scowl, the way it did when he embarked on his first studies of polynomial functions. After half an hour, Paul comes into the room. He kisses me when he sees my face, and Mom tells him there's ice cream and a Milano waiting for him in the refrigerator, though now it's a little melty. He goes to the kitchen and returns with the ice cream and cookie and eats it in the doorway while watching us draw.

"Yummmmmm," he says.

I work on my orbits. I create high-energy routes that could be taken by a chemically powered satellite that might detect and monitor and maybe destroy near-earth asteroids. Also, I try to relax my wrist. Up, down. Up, down. My son hums as he draws. Paul rattles his spoon. My mother's wrinkled hand flies over the page like a bird. She looks over at me, and our eyes meet. It's a workday, Monday, 4:00 PM, and we have nowhere to go. My family almost never spends this kind of time together, at least not unless someone is sick and we're all petrified. The sun comes through the window. The fires are under control. I realize that I love the stay-at-home-order, that I never want it to end, and that I'll remember this afternoon for the rest of my life.

Later that night, I reach for Paul in bed. He kisses me, in that old, soft, brushing manner, which begins at the mouth and ends at the hips. We laugh without making any sound as I bind my legs around his waist, in much the same way I once did in his college dorm room. I'm no longer able to swing myself into the shapes and enthusiasms that I could when I was a girl, but I can manage the long sway, the shudder, the grip of the hand on the jaw and a babble of filthy mumblings as we move together. Instead of chattering about the chemical composition of asteroids, or of the curious stability of Lagrange points, like we used to when we were young, we only stare at each other, tired and worn, while pawing and cuffing at each other. He reaches down and so that I might feel it there, and there, and, for a moment, I can.

Afterwards, he strokes my hair. I rest my head on his chest and close my eyes. I listen to him breathe.

"You were saying that you had a hard time, once," I say.

"Yes."

"Tell me what happened."

Paul rubs my shoulder. His chest moves up and down, slow and steady.

"I've told you about how my father died," he finally says.

I slip my arms around his waist.

"He had been walking through downtown Frankfort, on the way home from his school. It was a bad year. Morobe, one of our leaders, was in hiding. Botha had declared a state of emergency. But Frankfort is a smaller town, and we thought we were safe, as everything seemed to be happening in Johannesburg. The round-ups and the murders. And my father certainly wouldn't risk his own life, on account of his fears for my mother and me. All he was doing was coming home for dinner. A police officer saw him in the street and shot him in the chest. The man was a member of one of the death squads protected by Botha. I later learned that it took my father about an hour to die. There was no inquest, no charges brought. No trial, no sentence, no punishment. He was just killed, and nothing happened.

"Before that, I believed that a man's murder would mean something. When Sipho Mutsi was killed, we heard about that. And Andries Raditsela, Johannes Spogter. Meshack Mogale. I did not know that a person could be assassinated in broad daylight and his name would simply disappear. It didn't make any sense to me. It meant that life was meaningless.

"I stopped eating, as I told you. I refused drink. It was not a hunger strike. I simply ceased. My poor mother didn't know what to do. I didn't speak. I slept a great deal. Eventually, I developed pneumonia. My mother brought me to clinic, where they expected me to die."

I press my hot face to his arm and nod so that he'll keep telling me what happened.

"But she did not give up on me. She sat next to my bed. For days, weeks. She sat there and talked to me about my father. She reminded me. She would speak to me for hours, very calm, very friendly and joyful, as if we sat on a porch and chatted over a glass of tea. She reminded me of the things that he had taught me. Of the rocks and the crystals. How he had described to me the meteorite that had landed in Vredefort and blessed the land there. And how we had gathered the pebbles from that area, the basalt. How it was common knowledge among the people that the stones marked the place where the angel had alighted when the world was still new.

"She told me, and I remembered. Him. She and I knew that he had been murdered, I realized, and that was still something. And then I thought of all the families, the thousands and thousands and millions of people, who knew the same thing about someone they loved. A shooting here. A rape and murder there. A lynching, a strangling, a burning. They knew something terrible had happened to them. Something terrible had happened, but no one spoke of it because it was so ordinary, and so it was as if no one knew it at all. It simply was."

I am holding him so tight it probably hurts.

"This was not a nice thought, but it sufficed to get me out of bed. I walked out of the hospital and went back home. My mother cared for me. She fed me. She gave me herbs, wild sage and buchu. My coughing subsided. I gained weight. My eyes cleared. Shortly after that, I began to take my walks to Vrede-fort, to look at the dome.

"I'd walk all day and sit in the fields and stare out at the ring of hills. The olive trees branched against the sky. There is a species of wild hyacinth there, which I found quite lovely. Antelope would sometimes run across the bush and widowbirds flew in the air.

"Most of all, I gathered my rocks. I fingered the basalt in my pocket. It was as common as the grass. I found it in the crevices of the hills and inside birds' nests. It shone under the sun and stabbed the underside of my foot when it rolled inside my shoe. My father had said that it was a sign of the birth of the world. I had read about the impact that created the hills and saw that this ordinary stone spoke of ordinary things, being a violence so great the earth could never be the same. It was only later, when my colleagues fought me on my claims, that I realized only someone like him, and now like me, could understand this. It was a very lonely feeling. It remains so. A very cold, very solitary, very sad feeling."

Paul pauses, thinking, and kisses my wet face.

"And so, what?" I ask. "How do you get through it?"

Bronze light from the streetlamps drifts into the room. Outside it's quiet, except for the sound of traffic.

He smiles down at me. "You."

Eleven PM. Paul is flat on his back in bed, breathing loudly up at the ceiling, but I can't sleep and have come back to the living room. The pink pillow's nowhere to be found, but I'd picked up one of Tomás's sweatshirts in the hallway and am using that to anchor my computer on my lap. On the table next to the sofa sits a ceramic lamp painted with white flowers. I turn it on and a large, too-bright beach ball of light tosses into the space. When

I sign into Chrome, I whiz through my documents until I land again on the file dedicated to Gerald Wasserburg.

I click on a picture of Wasserburg that shows him sitting at a desk. A machine called the Lunatic I spectrometer squats in front of him. The device has a silver spoked wheel. Wasserburg turns it with his ivory hands. He wears glasses with black frames and lenses so thick that light pools in them, blanking out his eyes. A gray suit and white shirt bag on his frame, as if he can't keep on weight. He doesn't look like a combat veteran who's killed several people. But that had been when he was a teenage boy. This photograph shows him at age forty-two. His forehead travels far back into his hair and is notched in the middle, as if his big thoughts were stuck in the upper part of his head and had trouble getting out. This might almost make sense, considering how Wasserburg had to fend off antisemitism throughout his life and also the contradictions of rivals and enemies in the latter years of his career.

In the twentieth century, theorists had only begun to speculate about the goings-on in early space. In the 1920s Georges Lemaître conceived of the Big Bang and Albert Einstein wondered if the universe spun in a cycle in a kind of eternal return. In the 1950s Fred Hoyle imagined that all space was unchanging, without beginning and without end, and in the 1960s Harold Urey hypothesized that our world was born from a diamond-rich haze emanating from the sun. I don't know what was wrong with those men, such that they possessed that kind of imagination, but my studies have taught me that Wasserburg was one of them, a damaged person who could see what others couldn't. From his research, and his bad dreams, he discerned that long ago, when the solar system's planets were only fragile cakes of crust—iron and nickel and gas and dust—a swarm of massive rocks appeared out of the blackness and shot into them like bullets without end.

Our brief review of NEOs must also contend with the most sustained incidence of impacts in the earth's history, which we call the Late Heavy Bombardment (4.1–1.8 Ga). During this phase of geological history, Mercury, Venus, Earth and Mars faced an existential threat due largely to their diaspora from their original, serried configuration in space. The migration threw asteroids in the nearby Kuiper Belt into manic new trajectories, which sent them into collision courses with the four planets. For two billion years, the asteroids smashed into these bodies, forever changing their shapes, compositions, chemistries, and destinies. The Bombardment calls into question many things that human beings take for granted, even though they are mere fantasy: a permanent cosmos, for example, or the certainty of a continuing world. The risk that the Bombardment illustrates, however, may be beyond common comprehension, as it occurred during the Hadean period, an era so darkling and twilit that it is named after the Greek god of Hell.

Despite the eons that stand between then and now, we do have an idea of what occurred during the cataclysm. Our understanding hails from one Dr. Gerald J. Wasserburg, Caltech's

John D. MacArthur Professor of Geology and Geophysics (1927–2016). Before Wasserburg, no one could imagine the planets being battered in a constant dawn of magma and flame. Why could this man conceive of rampaging space when others could not? He was a sensitive soul. He had a friendless cast of mind. It also bears mentioning that young Wasserburg was no stranger to violence. Like many of his generation, he did not enjoy an uninterrupted educational career. Rather, after high school, he enlisted during the Second World War. Long before Wasserburg changed the planetary sciences with his theory, or began to ponder the catastrophes of the solar system, he had the bad luck of joining battle during the Prague Offensive in May of 1945. . . .

Keep your eyes sharp, Wasserburg, Sarge said, and then cursed him with a foul word. They were waist-deep in the freezing Teplá, the long green river glittering along western Czechoslovakia.

Wasserburg pushed his legs through the water. Overhead the sky was an ice blue. He spied a bird flying across the clouds. He looked down into the clear movement of the river, at the stones beneath the shimmer. He had loved such things once, at home in New Brunswick. Crystals and rocks.

Sir, he said, half-smiling with hate.

All of you, Sarge hissed over his shoulder at the men of the Second Division as they clattered toward the riverbank. Get ready to eat mud.

Wasserburg stared into the dark woods on the other side of the Teplá. He saw beech trees with naked-looking trunks. The black earth, painted with lime-colored leaves, showed no footprints, no candy wrappers or other junk.

No one here, he said. He held his rifle overhead, out of the wet.

They're in there, all right, Sarge said. You egg, you gink. You— Sarge called him a name, because he was a Jew. Stop yapping and get ready.

I'm sick, he said. His feet bled. He had a pain in his right side that hadn't let up for the past four days.

We're all sick, kid, Monroe said, behind him, laughing.

I need to go to the doctor.

Sarge hit him in the head with the butt of his rifle. He fell into the water.

You want another one? Doctor'll see you then.

I'm seventeen years old. He started crying.

Get up.

I see one, Monroe yelled.

Wasserburg looked toward the trees again. A shadow moved across the wood.

There! There! men screamed. The water turned white as they ran ahead.

He raced toward the trees. Everything cracked apart like a plate. The lime-green beech leaves fell with no sound. Men wearing the Germans' gray field dress fled. He aimed at their sprinting bodies. He saw a face. It was pink and white. He pulled the trigger. The face disappeared into the brush. Some-one, behind him, was begging. He understood. His grandfather had been from Vienna.

Ich habe eine Frau, ich habe eine Tochter, he heard.

He turned to see Monroe, with a knife, bending over a body. A black spray, as dark as the earth, stained the fog. Wasserburg was running again. The Sarge shouted. Other soldiers crouched and shot. He saw a German twist in the air as if broken in half by invisible hands. Two bodies fell, one after another. One had half a skull. The other had a dark hole in his throat.

He stopped, his lungs burning. The forest closed around him. He had strayed into an empty place. The woods went silent. But then, a movement. A shuffle; a twig crack.

He saw a flash of gray. The man, from before. Wasserburg raised his rifle and shot. The man sank between the trees. Red splashed up onto the victim's cheek. A neck wound. The man lifted his pink face, his mouth deformed with pain.

Ich habe keine Angst.

It was fine to hate them. But the blood got into Wasser-burg's eyes. He held onto his rifle.

Iche habe keine Angst! Ich habe keine Angst! Ich habe keine—

He pulled the trigger again. The face went in. The face went into the head. The man fell over.

Get him! Get him! Get him! he heard Sarge screaming.
He fell too, onto his side.

It did not look like anything, the killing. The Second Division
shot and hacked away at bodies. One German held onto the
spilling contents of his stomach while singing through his
teeth. A tall, thin corpse had collapsed into a bush, its legs still
jerking. Another German held a gun and wept. Beardsley, an
infantryman from Ohio, pointed his rifle and shot the crying
German in the chin, where an orchid appeared. Salamanca, a
Mexican from California, sawed at an old man who waved his
hands by his hips as if dancing.

Wasserburg stayed down. He stared at a rock sticking out
from the dirt, a small lump of black basalt. It reminded him of
pictures he had seen of Dachau, the burned bodies. A secret
knowledge entered his blood. He pressed his hands to his
eyes, trying to become blind. He pushed his right ear deep into
the mud, trying to become deaf. A long drop of spit fell from his
lower lip.

I lift my head. The house is quiet. Shadows cover the perimeter
of the living room like a stand of black trees.

Everyone in the house is asleep but me. It is 1 AM.

I begin typing again.

Almost thirty years after the war, in 1972, a shining silver contraption appeared above the moon. The CSM *America,* Apollo
17's spacecraft, jerked and tilted before landing in the thick dust
of the Taurus-Littrow valley. Dressed in his puffy white suit and
polycarbonate helmet, the astronaut Eugene Cernan drove out
of *America's* hatch, riding the Lunar Roving Vehicle as if it were
a plough. Cernan trundled onto the highlands of Earth's pale
satellite, gathering pebbles and small boulders. He collected

741 moon rocks and soil samples. Most of them were made of gray or black mare basalt, a rough and porous stone.

Apollo 17 went home.

After Wasserburg demobilized, he first sought refuge at Rutgers and then at the University of Chicago. He studied geology there because of his childhood interest in minerals and rocks. He had thrilled at the mysteries of quartz, thunder eggs, feldspar, rhyolites—trinkets he could pick up for free along the New Jersey rivers, as his family had no money to buy him toys. At school, he tried to get back that old innocence. But he also took classes under Zachariasen, Fermi, and Teller. He did well, and people took notice.

So people began to pay some attention to me, because it was unusual for somebody from a culturally deprived background like geology to get an A in physics, he later told an interviewer.

I was still very troubled—and I suppose I still am very troubled, always very threatened, for a variety of reasons. The war was not that far past, he said.

The war remained a thorn in his mind when Caltech hired him in 1955, and in 1972, when Apollo 17 landed in the Taurus-Littrow, his bad memories still had not gone away.

He set up shop in the Caltech basement. He labored there on his stones when he was not warring with his colleagues.

Leave me alone! he yelled at Leon Silver and Charles McKinney, whom no one remembers now.

All I want to do is work! he told them, over and over.

You have done nothing and published nothing! he went on.

I'm getting ulcers! he said.

When a sample of the highland rocks arrived from the Apollo mission, he sat down at his desk and stared at them as if they were his own newborns. The samples were tiny. Thin, precious slivers of mare basalt, like the parings of fingernails. The particles were too small to examine with existing technology.

He built a machine to study the moon rocks. He called it a mass spectrometer, but others nicknamed it the "Lunatic" after its maker, and called his basement workspace the "Lunatic Asylum." The Lunatic ingested the tiny specks of lunar basalt. It separated ionized particles from the fragments according to their masses. His assistants hovered close by, fretting in the murk of the laboratory. He ignored everything—hunger, exhaustion, the sibilance of his helpmeets' haggard breathing when he shouted. He was rewarded. The Lunatic coughed out its data. Uranium-lead dating showed a radical transformation in the rocks ~3.9 billion years ago.

We conclude that highland samples from widely separated areas bear the imprint of an event or series of events in a narrow time interval which can be identified with a cataclysm, he wrote in April 1974. He proceeded to author paper after paper, expanding his theory from a "lunar cataclysm" to the more shocking assessment that the entire solar system once suffered an unceasing asteroid attack.

At first, everyone believed his terrifying theory, perhaps because almost every researcher who had accomplished something in the field had been impaired by Hitler. Hordes of scientists gathered at conferences to debate the details. When he entered the dusty halls of Harvard, Brown, Princeton, and Yale, a hush descended on the room. He called his rivals crapheads and swore like those soldiers he'd hated, but instead of being branded a "lunatic," he found that his colleagues smiled and applauded him. He screamed at his secretary and threw his drinks across cafeterias, even while he won the Goldschmidt Medal, the Wollaston Medal, and the Crafoord Prize.

Yet slowly, as the years passed, the elites began to forget. Other wars began and ended, the Persian Gulf, Afghanistan, but they were fought by poor black and white men and seemed far away. His students crowded in his classrooms, belligerent and cocky, talking over his lectures. He could hear them whisper to each other that his ideas were fantastical, out of date. He pulled down his chalkboard and wrote out the math of it. The stones keep the secret knowledge, he tried to explain. They absorb everything, every terrible thing. One need only separate the ionized particles according to their masses.

One day, he entered a conference auditorium to find the younger men smirking. He climbed the steps to the stage and sat at a panel table, the fluorescent lights bouncing off his plastic name badge. A stripling with dark hair and acne simpered at him from the audience. The greenhorn raised his hand.

Do you really expect us to believe that this level of catastrophe could ever happen? the boy asked.

He looked down and said yes. There was the math of it, he should have emphasized. The dating of the uranium. The Lunatic's extreme precision. But he stammered and grew silent. He could not explain how he knew. How could he express that he had first seen evidence of the Bombardment long before the Apollo missions? That he had first glimpsed it when the forest branched before his eyes? There had been beech trees with lime-colored leaves. Men had run in the shadows, their throats gaping. The German he killed said that he was not afraid. Do you want another one? Sarge had hissed. Doctor'll see you then. He found it a very lonely feeling. A very cold, very solitary, very sad feeling. He could not show them, not tell them in any words, of his horror when he learned how bodies could collide and worlds might end. Or how he had seen his way through it.

6

The Lord of Chaos

Seven AM. I'm outside, wearing track shoes, shorts, and an old school sweatshirt. A mask presses under my chin. Tomás's wireless earbuds send me a stream of oldies music. My legs pump as I run on the sidewalk. I've slept five hours.

The sky is gold, with a fuchsia line flickering at the horizon. The air's still dirty but it's cool. Here's a dog walker on the other side of the street, bare-faced and reading her phone while her mammoth poodle lunges forward. I don't feel perfect operating on so little rest. When I first exited the house, it seemed like I could run for a solid hour, like I used to as a young scientist with a day off. But that fantasy ended after ten minutes. I have to take care of myself. And I have to schedule something sometime with a bone doctor. But it's nice out here so early, when the streets are quiet except for a few chirping birds.

Two blocks later, a male runner appears. He wears a mask over his mouth and nose. I pull mine up as he jumps off the sidewalk and crosses the street to get away from me. I wave and he waves back.

The sky gets lighter, bluer. Sweat clings to my face. A Latina carrying a black vinyl purse walks in the middle of the road, not looking at me, her face shielded below the eyes by a piece of daisy-patterned cloth. Even with the earbuds, I hear a chainsaw roaring from the end of the block. Other people show up, workers and neighbors. Some wear masks and some don't. A woman jogger with a long blond ponytail runs directly toward me, naked above the neck, smiling. I smile in return but get out of her way. I continue running until I have to stop, sooner than I want to. I bend over, press my hands on my knees, and fill my mask with gasps before turning around.

My chest is tight. I can feel the itchy outlines of my lungs. I haven't run even two miles and the effort makes me cough a little, but not a lot, not in a bad way. I turn around and head home, doing a serpentine to avoid human contact. When I return to our street, I see Paul framed by our house's kitchen windows. He's futzing around the stove, probably putting on coffee. I wipe my face on my sleeve and open the front door.

"Hey you guys," I say. "I'm back."

Once I'm in the shower, I cough two more times, getting rid of the smog I've let settle in my chest, but it still doesn't feel like a real cough, a dangerous cough.

By the time I get out and jam on my jeans and a fresh sweatshirt, my family's already making breakfast. In fifteen minutes, we're sitting down at the kitchen table, where my husband and son companionably battle to get the biggest portions onto their plates. Mom plays with some bread. I only look at my eggs because I guess adrenaline from my run has killed my appetite.

Tomás butters his toast. "So, we're going to the protest with Cecil and Blessica."

"Yes, like we talked about," Paul says. He seems tired this morning. There are deep wrinkles around his mouth. "What time does it start?"

"Eight," Tomás replies.

"Paul, honey, do you feel all right?" my mother asks.

He nods abstractedly and eats his potatoes.

"You look beat," I say.

"Just up late working."

My mother watches him closely. "Don't worry, he doesn't have it. He's not sneezing."

"It's coughing, not sneezing." I reach out and feel Paul's forehead. It's normal. "And he could have it and not know."

"I heard you in the shower, *you* sounded sick," Tomás says to me.

"I'm out of shape." I look at Paul. "Or do you think I should get a test?"

Paul gives me a wink. "Darling, being tired and wheezing a bit after running for the first time in ten years are normal things that happen. We just need to use common sense."

"If you ask me," Mom says, "I think this COVID's mostly the flu and people are going crazy right now."

I fill her cup with decaf because regular makes her blood pressure spike. "It's not a flu. Why does everybody keep calling it that? It causes organ damage."

Paul wags his head. "We're doing everything right."

I look over at Tomás. "Just remember that you're going to have to stay six feet apart from Cecil. And we have to wear masks."

"Got the memo, Mom," Tomás answers.

I pick at my scramble. The breakfast conversation develops into a discussion about the logistics for this evening, which are complicated by the protest how-to guides that my son's studied. He explains that we should hydrate before the action, write an emergency contact number on our bodies with Magic Marker, and download an ACLU app. Paul tells us how, in South Africa, he and his friends fended off police brutality by obeying all commands and pouring milk into their eyes when attacked with pepper spray.

"No, what you got to do with bad federales is run your ass off so they can't catch you," Mom says.

Why do they have to talk about this? It's making me see the night Paul was stopped by that police officer and his white shirt crumpled against the window when he spread-eagled against the car. While Paul begins to describe the effects of tear gas on the respiratory system, I feel a thin headache perching between my eyebrows. I don't want to remember how the policeman cursed at my husband while resting his hand on his gun, and I can't think about the possibility of Tomás choking. But I am. I look out the window and feel my head start to pixelate in a kind of self-hypnosis.

I nod like I'm listening but secretly tunnel down into myself. Down here, I drift, trying to focus on something pleasant. What comes up instead is Gerald Wasserburg. I picture his thick glasses, bulging forehead. Like my other stories, the account I wrote about him is fact, fiction, and incomplete. After World War II and his triumphs at graduate school, Wasserburg spent the entirety of his career at Caltech, where he picked fights over territory and attribution with the most important geologists in the field. He never recovered from the war. It gave him rare scientific insight but also isolated him from younger generations of academics, leaving him with only his family and a few acolytes for company. His findings disrupted our conception of the solar system as a static and self-monitoring system and introduced ideas of turbulence and death to subjects we prefer to think of as enduring. Like Einstein, like Newton, he dragged our understanding of space into modernity. But he didn't sit well with conflict. Wasserburg abandoned asteroid research and shifted into studies of the galaxy's chemical evolution when upstarts challenged his Bombardment thesis in long, combative articles that, at the time, threatened his legacy, though most of us still think that he was right.

I sift through my eggs with my fork while Paul details how gas damages the eyes. My thoughts skid over Wasserburg and fritz out like a broken TV set until I make them settle on another subject of my studies, Roy A. Tucker, the amateur who co-discovered Apophis and, in one important way, gave direction to my life. Tucker's a kind of son to the rest of my guys, I realize. I picture Tucker's bashful smile and nerdy spectacles, which I've seen in two photos. He doesn't look like a person who searches the skies for existential threats, though I suppose I don't either. He's tall, slightly chubby, pale, and resembles a math teacher or the owner of a used bookstore. To see him, you wouldn't guess at the fraternity he belongs to, or that he fought in one of our worst wars. Just like Wasserburg, Alvarez, and Kulik, he helped kill a lot of people and risked getting dead himself. I fiddle with the handle of my coffee cup, wondering about the events that might have wrecked Tucker badly enough that he became an asteroid hunter. Eventually, the images that come to mind so distract me that I thankfully can no longer quite catch what Paul's saying about chemical burns and blindness. I barely even taste my food when I eat it.

Once I finish the morning wash up, I text Blessica about tonight's meeting place and pack up some protest supplies, using a list that Tomás sent me from the Amnesty International website. Amnesty says to make an "eye flush" out of liquid antacid and water, so I stir up the mixture and pour it into a thermos. When that's done, I try to take a nap but just lie in bed, staring at the ceiling while my tension headache pulses behind the bridge of my nose. I finally climb out of my covers and put on shorts and one of Paul's T-shirts, then return to the backyard to continue my planting.

Out here, the lavender and poppies shine like jewels in the muck of the still-damp earth. I feel better outside. More alert, not so dried out. I grab my trowel and garden fork and chop up another bed, pouring new dirt in a layer on the ground. The day's still crisp. Sweat cools quickly on my skin. I dig holes and plant rows of marjoram, sage, and thyme. When the heat rolls in, I go back into the house to grab a wide-brimmed hat, which I find in the hallway closet. I continue digging and planting for hours, enjoying the light and even the filthy air—though the sage and thyme that I bought are mass-produced plants, factory farmed, and don't produce much scent.

Mom brings me water and a sandwich in the afternoon. I'm not hungry, but I drink. My arms and chest are slick with sweat. The heat burns beneath my eyebrows and collarbone. I keep digging, watering, fertilizing, and planting. I'm trying to hold onto that calm, I've-got-it-all-in-perspective feeling that came over me after I cried yesterday. This gardening is good, like the plumbing was for my kid. I find it's a hobby almost as absorbing as tracking Apophis at Goldstone or carefully planning out the next chapter of my "report."

Easing roots into the dirt, I regret that I've never met Roy Tucker. It's in large part because of him that I once collapsed in the JPL parking lot, looked up at the sky, and never was the same again. I've learned that he's sixty-nine years old, Anglo, an Arizonan, and came to astronomy in his own time and in his own way. Tucker qualifies as the most prolific contemporary discoverer of Near-Earth Objects, but I can't find much other information about him on the web. In one rare blog interview, Tucker did mention his Air Force tour in Thailand, which began in the last three years of the Vietnam War. I now know that Thailand was a dangerous spot when he first joined the military, especially at the U.S.'s Nam Phong Base. On Google Images, I've seen pictures of the manmade fireballs and shooting stars of 1972's Easter Offensive, otherwise known as the Nguyen Hue Campaign, which saw a massive army of North Vietnamese soldiers rolling into the demilitarized zone and attacking South Vietnam's "ring of steel." At Nam Phong, the U.S. called on the Air Force to cluster bomb the front. More than 100,000 North Vietnamese troops died during the Easter Offensive, along with tens of thousands of civilians and Southern soldiers.

I think that Tucker served in a support role for U.S. air operations from Nam Phong, based on my study of his expertise and the timing of his service. And I think, too, that he found the war some pretty rough going, though my theory is premised on slim evidence. In his interview, Tucker doesn't go into much detail about Thailand, but he does mention that his interest in asteroids began around the time of the offensive. I've written out all his quotes; they're in my phone, and I've nearly memorized a couple of them. *There wasn't a lot else to do in Thailand except go to work and read about astronomy,* he said. *So I read a lot of articles about asteroids.*

While I mull over what I've read about 1970s Thailand, and what Tucker said, I work on an aloe and move on to a pack of basil plants before I get to the cacti. These prickly pears leave little stickers in my skin, and I remove them carefully from their containers while piecing together a story about Tucker and his experiences as a soldier. But, after a while, the lack of sleep catches up with me. My mind softens down to a tired, hazy void. I let myself forget about my writing. My muscles ache, and I close my eyes, muttering to myself. A butterfly flickers over the aloe and I sit back on my haunches, trying not to worry about anything. I continue puttering around for a while longer, barely thinking much at all, and the day slips away from me. Soon enough the light turns dark gold, and I can hear the fireworks ramping up again. It's already time for me to clean up and get ready for tonight's protest.

Tomás stands next to his dad while holding his sign high in the air. He sings through his two masks.

Officers why do you have your guns out,
What are you following me for,
It's not real.

Hundreds of us gather on Sunset Boulevard. We all sing these phrases. They're the last words of unarmed Black people gunned down by police officers and, in one case, a vigilante, arranged by a composer named Joel Thompson a few years ago. My mother, husband, and son are on the sidewalk, six feet away from Blessica and Cecil. Tears run from our eyes and into our masks as we repeat these final things. The nightfall wraps itself around us. The shops are boarded up. Traffic lights fling droplets of green, red, and silver onto the crowd. All the people here give others the necessary space. I squint and exhale, as my forehead stings with an unhappy pressure.

To my right, Blessica stands in a dancer's posture. Her black hair hangs down by the sides of her face. She weaves her thin fingers together and holds them at her waist, as if she's singing in a church choir. She nods at me as I cry. Cecil's tall, looking nearly twice her size. He's wearing a scarlet T-shirt and puts his arm around her shoulders while calling something out to Tomás that I can't hear. Tomás stares back at the boy, his lover, and I can see everything he's feeling in his eyes. I turn away from them and sing. With one hand, I hold onto my thermos of eye wash. With the other, I push Mom's wheelchair. As the people call out, she raises her arms, half dancing, half conducting. Her gesture sets free the bell-like sounds of her bracelets.

The group walks down Sunset. Tomás and Cecil stride side by side, not too close together, up ahead. I keep my eye on the scarlet of Cecil's shirt. Paul keeps pace with them. My husband wears a white button-down and is easy to spot in the crowd on account of the tall shape of his head. My phone's lodged in my left pants pocket in case he gets too far away.

Mom is swiveling to take in everything while we all move slowly, one step or wheel roll at a time. To our sides, police officers scatter up and down the road, ignoring us, talking to each other. No one shouts in anger; no one threatens. I didn't know what to expect. I haven't protested before. I thought myself better used at Goldstone or Arecibo, where I could map the shapes of dangerous bodies that threaten us from the far distance. But as we walk, chants erupt behind me, and I add my voice. A thick, strong tenor calls out "What do we want?" The answers arrive.

Blessica takes my thermos. "We almost didn't come, but I'm glad we did."

"It's beautiful." My mother wipes tears from her eyes with both hands.

"I should have been out here before," I say.

"There are good reasons not to be," Blessica says. "They could get sick. They could get hurt."

We scan the crowd ahead, searching for our men.

"But the boys need it," Mom says.

"Yes," we agree.

The chants around us grow louder.

"Maybe things can change." Blessica holds the thermos to her chest. "I don't even know what's happening anymore."

"That's how I feel," I say. "That everything could flip on its head. From one minute to the next. But I don't know if the landing's going to be good or bad."

"Things are always flipping up and down," my mother says. "Everything's always good and bad."

"It's true," Blessica says, "but this feels different."

"Yes, it's different," I say.

"You young things," my mother says.

We walk. Blessica matches my stride. We chant Breonna

Taylor's name. We raise our fists. The pressure in my forehead doesn't lessen, but I concentrate on the people around me. One woman wearing a gray dress, and with her hair piled on top of her head, holds up a white sign I can't read. She runs on ahead, toward the front of the crowd. Different groups within the gathering yell demands. Recorded music sounds a deep beat up near where Paul, Tomás and Cecil march. Someone behind me starts the chorus of a gospel song. A few other voices join in, and I hear:

There is a balm in Gilead to make the wounded whole,
There is a balm in Gilead to heal the sin-sick soul,
Sometimes I feel discouraged and deep I feel the pain,
In prayers the Holy Spirit revives my soul again.

"I'm sorry about the other day," Blessica says, gesturing toward me. "About the food—"

A metallic noise swallows her voice. We turn to see. Close to us, gears grind and an engine bellows. People shout. A sound rises like a swell of water.

My mother is yelling my name. She's trying to stand up. The crowd behind us shudders and disassembles, first slowly, then in a frenzy. Blessica is tearing at me with her hands. I have my mother in my arms. People run past. A shot of pale smoke stains the air. A large black truck appears to our right. I'm away from my mother now. I slip and shove through the crowd. People peel off on both sides. Rushing in all directions. Faces and bodies flashing, disconnecting. A man dives in front of me, as if into the ocean, and lands on the asphalt. He doesn't move. Screams. The truck barrels on ahead.

I'm running. Can't breathe. Tear it off. The black helmets of police shine under the lights. An officer hits a man on the ground with his riot shield, over and over. I feel a punch on my shoulder. I run ahead. Where's Tomás? Everyone running faster. I am pushed. I fall onto the pavement, hitting my right hip, hard. I get up. Where's my mother? Paul? I turn around. No, I run back toward my son.

The black truck slams into the woman in the gray dress, the one carrying a white sign. Her head snaps, and she falls backward and forward at the same time, as if being pulled apart. She lies on the ground, motionless. The truck keeps going. Men run after it. I can't see Paul or Tomás. But I spot scarlet in the distance amid the grays and the golds and the blacks.

I run. I see only strangers. In my head I hear Paul say, *Stay in the car, Laura. Stay in the car.* Oh my God.

Burning on my cheek and wrist. I'm standing far up ahead on Sunset, alone. People flee down the road, though small clusters gather.

"Have you seen my son," I shout.

Two men look at me and shake their heads.

"His friend was wearing red."

A woman with a yellow bandana around her face points farther down the street.

I run now for a long time. I stop, shrieking as I try to catch my breath.

Far off I can see two people up on the street. Two young men. I see the scarlet. I race forward.

It's Tomás and Cecil, on the sidewalk. They lean into each other, their heads on each other's shoulders. Their arms wrap tightly around each other's backs. I take in my son's bare face, and then Cecil's. Their eyes are closed and they embrace. They are shaking.

"Being a mother's not a natural thing to do," Blessica says, an hour later. "I don't think that any person was built to handle this much pain."

Blessica and I sit on my back porch, maskless. I'm slouched down in my chair, stunned from a headache. Blessica cups her hands over her face. It's just us out here. My mother's gone to bed in horrified silence. Tomás and Cecil have disappeared into Tomás's room. Paul, ashen and with a ragged expression, has holed up in his office.

"No one ever talks about how hard it is, not really," Blessica stammers.

She'd been in bad shape after the truck hit the protester. Cecil had to hold onto her until she'd stopped screaming. I don't think I remember all of it. I'm not really sure how we all got back here, I was going insane, this migraine was keeping me from thinking straight.

"For a long time, I thought I'd never even become a mother," Blessica is saying.

I'm still seeing the woman get run over. I'm barely in my body and feel as if I'm running and running down Sunset.

"He came early," she goes on. "A couple days short of twenty-four weeks. A micro-preemie. Was your boy a preemie?"

She's gasping, chattering, crying.

"Sometimes, when they're born before twenty-four weeks, the doctors won't even try to save them. I have high blood pressure because of my genetics and they think that's why it happened. I was on bed rest when I started having Cecil. My husband was really good about it. I mean, my ex. Mark. We had a bad breakup but he's essentially a decent guy. With the baby, he didn't get worked up or anything. Except, I was bleeding. He called the ambulance. Mark kept saying, just hold on, just hold on, it's all right. But I knew that at not even twenty-four weeks, babies have a 50 percent chance. I had my hands on my stomach, and it was like, the fear. It's animal. I'd had miscarriages before. I had four miscarriages before my son. I don't know if you know what that means."

I reach out to hold her hand even though my head is blazing.

"When you have a miscarriage, you wonder how the human race could have continued this long. It only could go on because of men, you know? Men making women have sex. Forcing them to go through the consequences. Oh, I was hoping, and hoping, that my baby would be all right. Not be like the others. But everything was going so wrong. The doctors were quiet, and then they started yelling.

"They took him away. I didn't get to hold him or see him. I was on drugs and so everything was stolen from me. Mark was there, really pale, sitting in the chair next to me. The doctor came in and said there was a Grade 4 bleed. And an infection, which could be even more dangerous. And she said, even if he does make it, there could be problems, or there would be problems. 'Problems.' I knew what that meant.

"When I could finally move around a little, the nurse brought me to see him, through the window. He didn't look like a person, Cecil. More like an underwater thing. But I'd done a pediatric rotation. I'd watched the mothers and fathers leaving the hospital empty-handed. Mark said, to the nurse, 'This baby is going to make it.' And she didn't say anything. And I said to her, 'The baby might not make it.' And she said, 'Yes.'"

"Mark said, 'Our son's going to live.' But I didn't say that back. Maybe because I felt it more than he did? Or because I knew more because the baby'd been inside me? Or maybe because I'm a worse person than he is? Or because I'm stupider? I looked at my son, and he didn't seem like something that would survive. And I knew it would kill me if I wasn't prepared. So I said goodbye. Inside of myself, I said, 'Bye, baby.'" Blessica stares at me. "Do you think I'm a bad mother?"

I can't say anything.

"Because I am. I'm a bad mother. I can't forgive myself for saying that to him."

I take my hand from hers. I'm seeing black spots.

"Do you think I cursed him, saying that? Do you think I cursed us?"

"No, of course not," I force myself to say.

"I didn't, right?"

My throat is aching.

She touches her lips to stop them from trembling. "It's what I've worried about, ever since. And when, tonight—"

I stand up and move away from her while holding my forehead with my hand, trying to contain the throbbing. Blessica doesn't notice. She continues telling me her story, over and over. She glares into the silver sky, which swims with soot and ash. Above her fractured voice, I hear firecrackers, sirens, and shouts. The Bobcat Fire still burns twenty miles away. The space behind my eyes feels incinerated, torched like the black hills and black air of Los Angeles. I have made a mistake.

Dear Congress I have been asked to write §7 of the National Near-Earth Object Preparedness Strategy and Action Plan and herein please find a succinct synopsis

Congress I am writing this so as to inform you of the very real possibility that planet earth our home could at some point be liquidated by an asteroid that comes falling out of the darkness like Brother Death

But you cannot imagine it

even if you do read this report do you have the heart have you been so busted up so broken so wrecked so damaged that you can know what can really happen

Daer dongres as;kajsdfm soon we hae a have no system in place

I open my eyes. In the bedroom.

Heat drifts through me.

I hear someone. They're making terrible noises. It sounds as if their throat is being ripped apart.

It's my mother, coughing.

7

The Rose

It's night. In my bedroom. I don't know what day it is. I don't
know how much time has passed.

I was in the hospital, but I'm not anymore. Paul is sleeping
next to me.

How long was I gone?

I'm still not right. I might be drugged.

From out of the dark, images leap onto me like cats. I see
myself twisting, skinned by the pain.

I can't put it all together, what happened after I realized we
were sick.

I don't want to remember. My mind does it anyway.

I was having trouble breathing. There was something on me, I
couldn't get out from under it. A weight on my chest. I told Paul
to take it off, and he didn't understand.

I couldn't inhale.

Paul's eyes were naked and frightened.

I vomited, again and again. I heard the sound of my retching
coming from somewhere far away.

Paul held me as I flailed. My neck jerked. My head felt like it was cracking.

"Laura, they turned us away at the hospital, there's a surge."

"Where's my mother?"

"She's in the hospital. Darling, don't worry. I'm going to take perfect care of you."

"I want my mother. Where's Tomás? I can't breathe enough."

"I'll call the hospital again. But you have to drink. Drink. Drink. Drink. Drink this."

"Where's my mother?"

"Sweetheart, I can't hear you."

"Mother."

"I told you, she's in the hospital."

"Is she dead?"

"Drink this."

Paul's eyes were red. He forced the glass between my teeth. My teeth clattered hard enough to break it.

"Did I kill her?"

"Everything will be fine, everything's okay, you're going to be all right."

"Stay away from me."

He couldn't understand.

I turned my face away from him. "Stay away."

"You have to calm down. Please, please calm down."

Paul lifted me from the bed. I peed down my leg. There were red marks on my hands and my feet. My body was falling apart.

Then Tomás was in front of us. He was crying.

"Mom mom mom mom."

Paul, angry.

"Get out. Go to your room. You are not helping."
I opened my eyes. My son was gone.

Paul held my chin. The plastic bottle pressed against my lips.
Water ran down my face.

I crawled across the bed, trying to find a place where I could
breathe.

There was no day and night, only poison inside me.

My tongue was hot in my mouth and it had sores on it. My tongue
was too large and my eyes were too large and dripping down my
face. My head was on fire.
   It was all on fire. The fire was coming in heavy fuels.

Paul driving silently, speeding through the streets. I vomited in
the back seat until there was nothing left but dark blood and
thrashing.

Hospital. White shining into my eyes.
   They moved me onto a bed, and everything turned nasty and
violent. My body was rotten, I felt it crumbling on the inside.
   There was too much pain.
   I want my mother, is she alive.
   Where's Paul, where's my husband.
   "We can't allow any family, any visitors," someone said.

There were long stretches when I wasn't in my body, then I came
back again.
   I had an iv. A plastic mask gripped my nose and mouth.
   I opened my eyes and saw a nurse crying.
   "I can't work another shift, I can't do another one."
   I closed my eyes again.

Men stood above me.

"Hi there, Laura, we're going to just give you a little help with that breathing. We'll probably only have to intubate you for a few hours."

Paul where are you?

I don't want you to see

putting something in my

face

I felt dead. Something invaded me. Sliced its way down my tongue.

They took the tentacle out.

I didn't remember it, but my throat and mouth were pierced with lacerations.

I felt high. My mind was so soft, and I didn't care about anything. I reached down. A catheter. Even with the drugs it hurt bad, bad.

Two women stood above me. They wore plastic all over.

"You're doing so much better now, we're going to be able to release you in a day or two," one of them said.

"Where's my mother. Where's my husband and my son."

"Sorry, honey, I didn't catch that. Your voice isn't working that great yet."

The needle in my arm jammed in the wrong way. It stabbed me.

"Come again?"

I wanted to tell them about the needle, but instead I saw Paul at Caltech. He was laughing under the olive trees, and it was almost time for us to go to class. I explained how I had to write a story about Roy Tucker and put it in my report. I said, "I'm going to write a story about Roy Tucker so that Paul doesn't get cancer, because Dr. Skinner said we might have seen a few little changes but we think it's the trauma from the past surgeries and the biopsies and we'll also check back in three months."

One woman looked at the other woman.

"What did she say?"

"Nothing. It's the neurological sequelae."

I press my hands on my face, trying to blot out the memories. It's still dark. My husband continues to breathe deeply next to me.

It's the present moment. If there is such a thing.

Don't think about it anymore.

Relax, get better. Sleep.

Sleep now.

But I can't because I had visions in the hospital. I can see them in fragments.

I was as crazed as a prophet.

Paul

remember how I fell in the parking lot
remember how roy a tucker found apophis the Egyptian death god
the enemy of the sun god Ra
roy tucker
looks for killer rocks for fun why do you think he would do that it's
not a normal thing
let me tell you why he does that
because I understand
there wasn't a lot else to do in Thailand except go to work and read
about astronomy
So I read a lot of articles about asteroids

that's what he said
it's like he was trying to tell me something.

ladies and gentlemen of the united states congress a report on the
history of meteorite impacts would be incomplete without a small
chapter on roy a tucker the man who discovered the asteroid apophis
on a dark day in june of 2004 when he looked through the telescope
and saw a smear a white blur a fuzzy ball an asteroid as large as three
football fields falling down on us

roy a tucker
he lives in Arizona he is old looks harmless but I researched him I
know that he knows

The Rose

what can happen

and how that knowing will kill you

unless you can see through it

he said he joined the air force in 1972 he was in Thailand
what did roy a tucker do in Thailand that easter
easter offensive
one hundred forty thousand dead . . . .

the soldiers stomped into the barracks drinking   laughing about
the mission
joyously screaming obscenities about body counts
wrestling   faces bright   singing songs about the corpses in the
mud
he sat in a corner his face drained   he was reading a book
the men came over   cuffed him   roused
him   joking   tearing it out of his hands
why are you reading about outer space? they said   slapping
through the pages
he raised his dead eyes and told them,
all it takes is a rock one klick across it could kill everything
they looked at each other
a rock that size would kill all the vc and also you and you and you
and you and me, he said
what are you talking about, they laughed
the end of the world   it could happen anytime,
he explained
they made faces   turned away from him
what the hell is wrong with that guy
he took back his book
and asked,
Do you think we cursed ourselves?
but they ignored him   drank and rejoiced   over the dead

I look over at Paul. His back is toward me. He is curled into himself and wrapped up in the covers.

I squeeze my eyes to shut out the ghosts of my insanity. It doesn't work.

I don't feel like the same person anymore.

I want to wake Paul so he can tell me everything is going to be all right. That what I saw in the hospital was just the virus playing tricks on me.

I know if I move he will rise with a start and do anything I ask.

But no, he can't help me.

I open my eyes. Morning. Paul is gone.

The painkillers they gave me are lifting. The sickening replay of the hospital has stopped. My chest and throat feel burned. I look out the window. The sky shines bright yellow. It's as bright as a rain jacket.

Time passes in a strange way. I can think and then I can't think.

Paul stands by the bed. His face glows, he's healthy and beautiful. This makes me ashamed.

"Mother?"

I am hissing. My tongue is sore and too large in my mouth. My throat is flayed.

"She's in the hospital, sweetheart," Paul says.

"Die?"

"They're hoping to take her off the machine soon, maybe tomorrow."

"Tube?"

"Yes."

"Tomás?"

"Both of us just had mild symptoms. We're fine."

"Where?"

"He's sleeping."

"Mother die?"

He bends down and kisses me all over my face.

"We don't know."

Awake again. I look down. I see a crumpled pillow and a whipped-cream burst of sheets. My legs stick out from the whiteness. They're thin and loose, like a bundle of rags. They're bruised. This is a stranger's body.

I can't eat solid food. My tongue has rough red wounds. They're healing. I drink some sort of shake. It's pink and smooth.

I taste nothing. But the liquid goes down my throat cold and soothing, which is a blessing.

Paul brings me my computer. As he places it on my legs and plugs it in, I see his quivering mouth.

"You're tired." My voice is not healing. It shivers and splinters.

He leans over and touches my face with both hands. He's crying.

"I love you," he says.

For one day, I lie in my bed with my hand on the smooth silver shell of my computer. My eyes open, then close.

I slide in and out of my mind. I can't work.

I am stronger.

I write and call the manager at my Trader Joe's and the staff at Saint Joseph's, where I had my scans. They can barely understand me because of my voice, but I think they get the message that I might have gotten them sick.

When I'm online, I see that four days ago, Somnang emailed me.

Dear Laura,

Re our findings at GS, I've been emailing David Tholen, who believes that Apophis will need another look. It appears to be sliding off its trajectory. Thus a 2068 impact cannot yet be ruled out.

I'm sorry to say that I've been feeling a bit under the weather and will get myself seen by my physician. Will let you know the results when I hear.

I email Somnang. I call him. He doesn't answer the phone. When I email and call his assistant, Advay, I also can't reach him.

I sleep and wake. I go to the bathroom. I sleep.

My mouth hurts less. I don't look at it or at my face in the mirror.

On a morning when I can keep my eyes open, I look through my files. I'm shaking. My mouth hurts again.

I stare at my documents, sifting through their many words. In the hospital, I'd thought I grasped something important. This important thing was about Roy Tucker.

During my earlier research, I'd learned that during the Easter

Offensive, the U.S. used combat planes like the *Republic F-105 Thunderchief*, which dropped cluster bombs on the enemy and also civilians. I'd clicked on and enlarged pictures of the attacks. I shifted back and forth between these bright, almost abstract photographs and Tucker's interview, where he described reading about asteroids in Thailand because there was nothing else to do but work. At my sickest, the images of lands that had been burned and flattened by U.S. bombs exploded inside me, a hallucination that didn't seem to stop for days.

I click on the file containing my draft notes for the *National Near-Earth Object Preparedness Strategy and Action Plan* history section. My writings on Kulik, Hodges, Alvarez, and Wasserburg spool across my screen. I reread them.

I realize that I'm more like my mother than I thought.

Tomás comes into my room. He stands far away from me, by the door. He's gaunt, but his body moves easily, without pain. His face trembles.

"Mom."

"It's okay," I rasp.

"What if I get you sick again?"

"Come here."

"But maybe I'll get you sick again. And you'll be like Grandma."

"Come here."

"But Grandma's so sick, and you could be too."

"Dad told me. Off that machine. Getting better. Spoke to doctor yesterday. See her soon."

He crawls into bed as if he were a little boy. He presses his face into my stomach and cries into it.

"I'm sorry."

"No."

"Does it hurt?"

"No." I remember something. "Cecil and mom?"

"They both got it."

"Bad?"

"They didn't have to go to the hospital." He begins crying again. "But she won't let him talk to me."

He cries some more. I touch his hair and his cheeks. I kiss him.

"You didn't do this." An image of my mother flashes into my mind, the darkness of her eyelids and the beauty of her hands. "It was me."

Election night. Paul helps me bathe for the big occasion and I put on a fresh nightgown. All three of us cuddle in bed and watch CNN on my computer. Paul drinks beer and Tomás drinks an orange soda. I have half a pink protein shake. Since being discharged from the hospital, I've had almost no medical guidance from my doctors about how to care for myself, but protein seems like a good idea because my body's wasted. The nurses did say not to talk too much, indicating that my vocal cords are in danger.

My computer screen flashes red and blue. Men and women speak very loudly and rapidly about Wisconsin, Arizona, Pennsylvania, North Carolina, Michigan, Georgia, and Nevada.

Paul puts his hand on my left leg, and Tomás grasps my right arm. I look down to see that they both have the same long pianists' fingers. Paul has no musical ability. But I think about Tomás's sketch, the one he made when he and my mother and I drew orbits or roses in the TV room. Mom had complimented the perfection of his line. If she died, he wouldn't have her in his life, and I know he needs her.

While studying Georgia on CNN's map, I fall asleep.

A History of Hazardous Objects

For hundreds of years, astronomers assumed that asteroids could not move into the Earth's orbit because no one had ever observed such a phenomenon. On August 13, 1898, Carl Gustav Witt, Felix Linke, and Auguste Charlois became the first planetary scientists to document 433 Eros, a verified Earth-crosser. Since that time, over 25,000 Near-Earth Asteroids (NEAS) have been discovered, and, of these, 1,489 qualify as Potentially Hazardous Objects (PHOS). Conservatively, unidentified neas number in the dozens.

While doing research for this study, this reporter learned that the broad scientific community had long denied any risk of Earth experiencing a catastrophic meteorite collision, while a small cohort of geologists, physicists, and astronomers knew otherwise. Some of these experts shared the experience of enduring combat in one of the wars of the twentieth century, and during these episodes they either found themselves under fire or killed the enemy with bombs and other deadly projectiles. It appears that members of this small brotherhood made sense of the torment they sustained and caused by adapting the lessons learned in the theater of war to the threats posed by the great rocks of space:

Dr. L. Kulik (Russia, b. 1883, Estonia), who withstood firsthand exposure to blast waves in the Russo-Japanese war, traveled to Tunguska, Serbia, in 1927 to record the effects of the meteoritic shock that destroyed much of the area in 1908.

Dr. W. Alvarez (American, b. 1911), whose work at Los Alamos led to the dropping of "Fat Man" onto Nagasaki in 1945, later co-led a mid-1970s investigation concluding that a meteorite 7–10 km in diameter detonated on Earth 66 million years ago and caused a worldwide extinction event.

Dr. G. Wasserburg (American, b. 1927) joined battle on the Czechoslovakian border during the waning days of World War II. His experience under fire and the terrors of the Holocaust were thereafter echoed in his theory of the Late Heavy Bombardment, which posits the solar system's history of annihilation and violence.

Roy A. Tucker (American, b. 1951) may have aided the U.S.'s campaign to saturate bomb the North Vietnamese during the last years of the Vietnam War, only to later co-locate 99942 Apophis, an Empire State building-sized Earth-crosser that some astronomers fear will eventually collide with our planet.

These stories, which detail the relationship between trauma and scientific discovery, permit us to wonder if mankind's endurance of evil and suffering might invest in us the wisdom necessary to better understand and protect one another. That is, could man's ample inheritance of worldly sorrow lead us to some higher meaning? Sadly, the example of A. Hodges (American, b. 1923), the only known human being to have direct contact with a meteorite, suggests otherwise: The injuries she received from the nine-pound "Hodges Meteorite" frayed her ability to reason, causing her to descend into a mental illness from which she never recovered.

NASA's study comes to Congress during a political moment roiled with a pandemic, the rise of tyranny, environmental collapse caused by human-created climate change, a surfeit of state-sanctioned and race-based violence, and the numerous worries that accompany these ills. While this reporter finds her share of optimism so exhausted that she can barely dare to hope, she still recognizes the possibility that these ordeals could inspire us to build a more sensible world. It is in a combined spirit of despair and longing that this reporter recommends the development of a comprehensive PHO detection, deflection, and/or destruction system, in order to secure our already-fragile globe against the slim but important risk of a consequential impact by space object.

As will be set forth in §18, many possibilities for such

an enterprise exist, though one of the most feasible would be premised on the launching of Earth-returning satellites programmed to orbit nearby neighborhoods. These satellites might travel around our planet in semicircular routes. Their trajectories would form a rounded, overlapping matrix that characterizes classic sentinel schemas. When mapped, this pattern expresses such delicate beauty that some observers describe it as a "rose."

I edit my report and email it to Somnang, care of Advay. This time Advay writes me back almost immediately and confirms that Somnang has been stricken with the virus. My boss is in the hospital. I send Advay my regrets and write Somnang a lengthy letter of condolence and apology. I don't know how I got the virus, but I'm sure I gave it to him at Goldstone.

I email letters of apology to Blessica and Cecil.

I look at the news. It's December 13, a Sunday. The first shipments of vaccine are being delivered to hundreds of sites across the country. A small group of Trump supporters have rallied in D.C., holding a protest that turned violent, with several stabbings. Biden's won, but Trump still hasn't conceded.

I pick up my phone and dial the number of the Keck Medical Center in downtown Los Angeles, where doctors now treat my mother for complications from SARS-COV-2. It's the same hospital that treated me. I leave my message for Mom's attending nurse, a tired-sounding woman named Jean, who's given me a direct extension. I know that Mom got off her ventilator four days ago but remains in the ICU. I can't visit her because of the new policies implemented by medical facilities since April. I've called her many times, but, as of three days ago, she remained unconscious. I tried to find out her status yesterday and the day before but didn't reach anyone who could tell me this information.

After I leave the message, I lean my head back on my pillow

and look at spots of light playing on the wall. They look like gold leaves, rustling. I fall asleep.

The phone rings.

"She's awake," Jean says, in her gravelly voice. Jean didn't treat me when I was at Keck, and so I don't know what she looks like, but I recognize her voice immediately.

"Can I talk to her? Right now?"

"Not yet."

"Can I come visit her?"

"No. Too dangerous. Only phone visits allowed right now."

"When?"

Jean pauses, thinking.

"I think tomorrow."

I manage to take my first walk around the house. The computer says that I have to move, to prevent pneumonia and blood clots, so I trudge up and down the corridor. Paul and Tomás try to prop me up, but I tell them that I'm fine, and am just "getting a little exercise."

I walk to the living room and sit on the couch, breathing hard. I walk to the kitchen and sit at the table, thinking about those stories I couldn't help but write.

I walk to the TV room. My mother's drawings and paintings still lie scattered over the sofa and on the floor. I lower myself to the carpet and touch the papers. I stroke my fingers over the dark swirls, the streaks of blue, of fuchsia, pink, canary yellow, and the purple and the orange together.

I can't sleep all night, thinking of her.

The next day, Paul, Tomás, and I huddle together on the big bed, looking at the masked and plastic-guarded face of Nurse Jean on my phone. She stands outside my mother's room, against a white wall. A surgical cap covers her hair. Her neck and face appear wide and fleshy. The clear plastic of her face shield reflects shards of fluorescent light. I can barely see her eyes.

"I can hold up the phone, and you can talk to her," she says. "She's awake, though I don't know for how long."

In the phone's screen, I can see not only Jean but also a small video square that shows my husband, son, and me. I look ancient.

"How is she?" My voice is better but still weak.

"She's off the ventilator," Jean says.

"I know, but how is she doing?"

"It's a good sign that we could take her off."

"Is she going to live?"

Jean moves her head so the flashes of light fly across her face shield.

"We're going to have to wait and see," she finally says. "Wait and hope for the best."

I don't say anything.

"Sugar, that's just how it is."

"Am I saying goodbye to her right now?"

Jean's voice cracks. "I don't know, honey. Some people pull right through. But prayer's a good idea, too."

"Mom," Tomás says.

"She can't tell you anything different," Paul says. "She's not going to say that everything will be all right, because if it isn't, we might sue the hospital."

My whole body feels tight, disconnected, and unreal.

"Let me talk to her, please."

Jean moves into the ICU. It's a gray and white place, crammed with machines and people. I hear men and women giving terse orders for blood draws and sedation.

Jean walks into a private room. She turns the camera around. I see my mother, small and shriveled in a bed. She's attached to metal boxes and tubes. Her head is thrown back and her mouth is open. Mom's glamorous silver hair is hidden under her blue cap. Her withered throat descends into a white cotton gown decorated with pink rosebuds. Her wasted arms are blue and red, bruised from the IVs. Her eyes look erased. She looks like she's wearing violet lipstick, but it's not lipstick, it's the color of her lips. Her eyes flutter open.

"Go to the other room," I say to Paul and Tomás. "She doesn't want you to see her like this."

Tomás unwinds himself from me. He stands up, gripping his hands together. Paul kisses my cheek. They leave, quickly, and close the bedroom door behind them.

"Isabel?" Jean says.

"It's Isabella," I say.

"Isabella, it's your daughter, she wants to say hey to you, honey."

My mother looks into the phone, not understanding.

"It's me, Mom," I say.

"It's your daughter," Jean says.

"Right here, Mom," I say.

She looks into the screen. I don't know if she can see me.

"Mama," I say.

"Her throat might be a little tender right now," Jean says. "Might be better if you do most of the talking."

My mother breathes slowly and carefully, staring almost sightlessly into the phone.

"It's me, Mom."

"That's good," Jean says. "I can do this for a couple minutes. You two say hey and catch up."

We look at each other through the phone. Her face is utterly changed. Her cheek and jaw bones jut out like knuckles. She struggles to speak.

"Don't." I force my voice out. "It's okay. You don't have to talk. I'm here. I'm here. I'm here. I'm right here."

She nods.

"I'm here with you, Mom. I love you, Mom."

She strains to say my name, but all that comes through is air.

"I love you," I say.

The outward corners of her eyes tilt downward in a way I've never seen before.

"You're beautiful, Mom."

Her cheeks tremble.

"You were always beautiful. As long as I can remember. The most beautiful woman in the world."

She purses her lips. I know she is trying to say *you.*

"Always, always the most beautiful. Even as a little girl. Since the day you were born. You're special, Mom. Been that way your whole life."

My mother gazes at me, her mouth slack.

"Even as a little girl, back in Chicxulub, you weren't just a pretty face. You could draw anything. You could draw a tree, you could draw a cloud, you could draw a house, the ocean, a fish, a star, the moon. And roses, too.

"You were beautiful, but what you cared about most was your art. You were going to be an artist. You tried to study art, in books. And these books said, you have to draw before you can paint. You have to master one art before you can master another. So that's what you did. You drew the roses that grew wild in the back of your house, but you never painted them, because you didn't think you were ready."

She closes her eyes and opens them again, breathing hard.

"Soon enough, though, your drawings became better and better, so good that people couldn't understand them. Your neighbors looked at them and said, 'I liked the other ones more,' and 'That's not a rose! What are you thinking?' But you knew you had to keep at it, to make them perfect, until you finally could paint them. That day didn't come for a long time.

"When you were sixteen years old, George Vincent Brooks

came to your mother's house, with money and one red rose. When you first saw the flower, you were happy, because you knew what you'd do with it. But George Vincent Brooks didn't bring you a rose for drawing.

"Your mother smiled and flirted with him. Soon, she left and came back with a bottle of liquor. Brooks and your mother settled in for a long time, drinking and talking, and your mother told you to leave. You didn't understand, but you were so young that you didn't think any more about it.

"Two days later, Brooks came back. This time he didn't bring roses. Your mother said you had to go with him. They said you were going to get married. When you started to cry, your mother shouted at you, and she beat you. 'We are starving to death,' she said. You went with him. You wanted to bring your papers and pencils, but Brooks said that he would have everything you needed. You insisted on bringing your drawings, at least, and then you left your house, not sure what to do or what to believe. Though he seemed nice. He liked red wine. He wanted you to like it too. You drank with him. It made you feel happy, to be drunk.

"When Brooks hit you for the first time, in the stomach, you thought it was a mistake. But then it happened again, and again, and you realized what he was. You ran to Abuela and begged her to help you, but she said you were a drunkard who had brought shame on the family. That's when you remembered the old story of Brother Death falling through the air. And that's how it seemed, that you were falling and falling."

My voice is thinning down to static, but I will keep talking to her until it disappears.

"On the day you realized that you were pregnant, Brooks hit you until you had blood in your mouth. You sat up night after night, crying. You knew what would happen to me if you stayed and what could happen to us if you left. It almost killed you. But, somehow, you saw your way through it.

"One night, while Brooks slept, you crept out of bed. You took the money, your wedding license, and your drawings. And you ran. You ran all the way here, suffering so much along the way, and once you got here, too. The States weren't the good place you had heard about. But you did it. You did it to save me, Mom."

My mother looks at me, her eyes filmy and her lips parted. Tears roll down her cheeks and soak the front of her gown. Her throat works hard.

I watch her lips move, but I can't hear anything.

I press my fingers to my phone's screen, touching her face.

"Yes," she whispers.

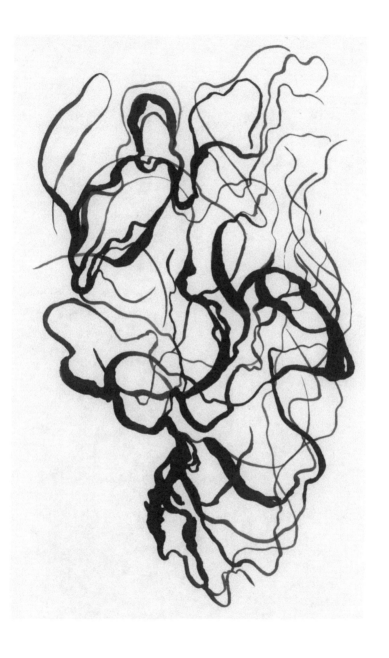

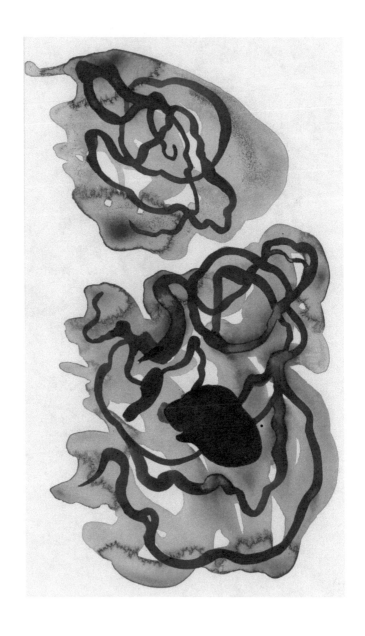

Notes and Sources

In the fall of 2020, David J. Tholen, one of the co-discoverers of Apophis, reported new data about Apophis that created concern. Tholen's updated assessments derived from his calculations concerning the "Yarkovsky effect," the name for the influence the sun's rays have upon a passing asteroid. His studies indicated that the force of the sun's energy may be causing Apophis to meander. At a presentation at the American Astronomical Society's Division for Planetary Sciences, Tholen reiterated that Apophis would not strike Earth in 2029, but he noted that 2068 might be a different story. Those new observations of Apophis, he said, showed "that the asteroid is drifting away from a purely gravitational orbit by about 170 meters per year, which is enough to keep the 2068 impact scenario in play." *See,* "Massive asteroid subject of new findings." *University of Hawai'i News* (October 26, 2020), https://www.hawaii.edu/news/2020/10/26/new-massive-asteroid-findings/.

However, in March of 2021, the European Space Agency removed Apophis from its "risk list" of potentially hazardous objects based on yet newer data obtained at Goldstone. *See,* "Asteroid Apophis impact ruled out for at least a century." *Astronomy*

Now (March 26, 2021), https://astronomynow.com/2021/03/26/asteroid-apophis-impact-ruled-out-for-at-least-a-century/.

In April of 2021, NASA conducted a drill wherein it attempted to deflect a hypothetical asteroid heading toward Earth, based on a lead time of six months. It failed. *See,* McFall-Johnsen, Morgan, and Aylin Woodward. "A NASA simulation revealed that 6 months' warning isn't enough to stop an asteroid from hitting Earth. We'd need 5 to 10 years." *Business Insider* (May 12, 2021), https://www.businessinsider.com/nasa-asteroid-simulation-reveals-need-years-of-warning-2021-5.

Puerto Rico's Arecibo, one of the two radar telescopes capable of imaging minor planets, collapsed on December 1, 2020. Its future is uncertain. *See,* Witze, Alexandra. "Gut-wrenching footage documents Arecibo telescope's collapse." *Nature* (December 2, 2020), https://www.nature.com/articles/d41586-020-03421-y. As of 2023, it was reported that the the observatory was "pivot[ing] to an educational mission." *See,* Lloreda, Claudia López. "As famed Arecibo Observatory shuts down, its scientists face an uncertain future." *Science* (July 12, 2023), https://www.science.org/content/article/as-famed-arecibo-observatory-shuts down-its-scientists-face-an-uncertain-future.

Roy A. Tucker died on March 5, 2021, the same week that Apophis had a close fly-by. *See,* Beatty, J. Kelly. "Asteroid Apophis pays earth a visit this week." *Sky & Telescope* (March 5, 2021), https://skyandtelescope.org/astronomy-news/apophis-pays-a-visit-this-week/.

Later that summer, NASA approved the development of a space telescope that will be dedicated to the detection of Near-Earth Objects. *See,* "NASA approves asteroid hunting space telescope to continue development." *Jet Propulsion Laboratory* (June 11, 2021), https://www.jpl.nasa.gov/news/nasa-approves-asteroid-hunting-space-telescope-to-continue-development.

On September 26, 2022, NASA's Double Asteroid Redirection

Test (DART) intentionally collided with the asteroid Dimorphos and successfully altered the asteroid's orbit. "This marks humanity's first time purposely changing the motion of a celestial object and the first full-scale demonstration of asteroid deflection technology." *See,* Bardan, Roxana. "NASA confirms DART mission impact changed asteroid's motion in space." *NASA* (Oct 11, 2022), https://www.nasa.gov/press-release/nasa-confirms-dart-mission -impact-changed-asteroid-s-motion-in-space.

A History of Hazardous Object's "Section Seven" of the *National Near-Earth Object Preparedness Strategy and Action Plan* is based in part on NASA's *2006 Near-Earth Object Survey and Deflection Study,* https://www.hq.nasa.gov/office/pao/FOIA/NEO _Analysis_Doc.pdf.

Paul's theory about basalt is a riff on D.E. Moser, et al's theory that gabbronorite found in the Vredefort Dome may derive from a meteorite's impact. I substituted basalt for gabbronorite in order to prevent piggybacking too much on their controversial argument. *See,* Mayne, Paul. "Crater discovery's impact echoes still today." *Phys.org* (May 23, 2014), https://phys.org/news/2014-05-crater- discovery-impact-echoes-today.html. *See also,* Cupelli, C.L., et al. "Discovery of mafic impact melt in the center of the Vredefort Dome: Archetype for continental residua of early Earth crater- ing?" *Geology* 42, no. 5 (April 2014), https://www.researchgate .net/publication/263776269_Discovery_of_mafic_impact_melt _in_the_center_of_the_Vredefort_dome_Archetype_for _continental_residua_of_early_Earth_cratering.

Vasily Okhchen's Evenki insults are taken from the papers of Theophilus Siegfried Bayer (1694–1738), transcribed by David Weston. *See, An Evenki Vocabulary from the Papers of Theophi- lus Siegfried Bayer,* https://www.gla.ac.uk/media/Media_489484 _smxx.pdf.

The July 2020 study of Huoshenshan Hospital that Laura refers to is by Guo, Zhen-Dong, et. al. "Aerosol and surface distribution of Severe Acute Respiratory Syndrome Coronavirus 2 in hospital wards, Wuhan, China, 2020." *Emerging Infectious Diseases* 27, no. 7 (July 2020), https://wwwnc.cdc.gov/eid/article/26/7/20-0885_article.

The study of COVID's spread in nursing homes is found in Chen, M. Keith, et al. "Nursing home staff networks and COVID-19." https://arxiv.org/abs/2007.11789, (working paper, July 22, 2020), https://arxiv.org/abs/2007.11789, later published in *PNAS* 118, no. 1 (January 5, 2021).

Dr. Wannian Liang and Dr. Bruce Aylward's findings regarding household transmission of the SARS-COV-2 virus are found in "Report of the WHO-China Joint Mission on Coronavirus Disease 2019 (COVID-19)." (February 2020): 16–24, https://www.who.int/docs/default-source/coronaviruse/who-china-joint-mission-on-covid-19-final-report.pdf.

The study of the effects of the lockdowns on parents is found in Fontanesi, Lilybeth, et. al. "The effect of the COVID-19 lockdown on parents: A call to adopt urgent measures." *Psychological Trauma: Theory, Research, Practice, and Policy 12, no. s1* (2020): S79–S81, https://ricerca.unich.it/retrieve/handle/11564/730961/212189/2020-41430-001.pdf.

The police and hate violence at the protest described in this novel are inspired by real events that occurred in Los Angeles in September 2020. I have changed dates, some key facts, and merged two episodes of state and vigilante violence against protesters. *See,* Mansell, William. "2 vehicles hit protesters in Los Angeles as Breonna Taylor protests continue throughout US." *ABC News* (September 25, 2020), https://abcnews.go.com/US/vehicles-hit-protesters-los-angeles-breonna-taylor-protests/story?id=73234687. *See also,* Paskin, Julia. "Sheriff's Dept. uses force at Breonna Taylor protests in West Hollywood." *LAist* (September 26, 2020), https://laist.com/news/breonna-taylor-protests-day-3.

Other works of reportage, history, scholarship, and music that informed the writing of the book are:

Dolan, Jack, and Matt Hamilton. "Would elderly be safer at home? L.A. health czar says it's time to consider taking loved ones out of nursing facilities when possible." *L.A. Times* (April 7, 2020), https://enewspaper.latimes.com/infinity/article_share .aspx?guid=882613a1-8a54-4735-b949-7fa5a0796496.

Osborne, Lucy. "Donald Trump accused of sexual assault by former model Amy Dorris." *The Guardian* (September 17, 2020), https://www.theguardian.com/us-news/2020/sep/17/donald -trump-accused-of-sexual-assault-by-former-model-amy -dorris (this provides the source material for the italicized quote by Amy Dorris).

George, Alice. "In 1954, an extraterrestrial bruiser shocked this Alabama woman." *Smithsonian Magazine* (November 26, 2019), https://www.smithsonianmag.com/smithsonian-institution /1954-extraterrestrial-bruiser-shocked-alabama-woman -180973646/ (this provides the source material for the italicized quotes by Ann Hodges, which are slightly modified).

Trower, W. Peter, ed. *Discovering Alvarez: Selected Works of Luis W. Alvarez with Commentary by His Students and Colleagues.* Chicago: The University of Chicago Press, 1989 (this provides the source material for the italicized quotes by Luis Alvarez).

Note that the "Alvarez hypothesis" is attributed not only to Luis Alvarez but also Walter Alvarez. Frank Asaro and Helen Michel also participated in the development of the theory. For the real story of the Alvarez hypothesis, *see* Yarris, Lynn. "Alvarez theory on dinosaur die-out upheld: Experts find asteroid guilty of killing the dinosaurs." *Berkeley Lab* (March 9, 2019), https:// newscenter.lbl.gov/2010/03/09/alvarez-theory-on-dinosaur/.

Valone, David A. "Gerald J. Wasserburg (1927–2016) (April 25, May 3, 10, and 17, 1995)," https://oralhistories.library.caltech .edu/246/1/Wasserburg%20OHO.pdf (this provides the source material for the italicized quotes by Gerald Wasserburg). The scenes of the young soldier Wasserburg fighting in Czechoslovakia are inspired by this interview.

Tera, Foad, D. A. Papanastassiou, and G. J. Wasserburg. "Isotopic evidence for a terminal lunar cataclysm." *Earth and Planetary Science Letters* 22, nos. 1–21 (April 1974), https://www.sciencedirect .com/science/article/abs/pii/0012821X74900594?via%3Dihub (this provides the source material for Gerald Wasserburg and his team's italicized quote regarding the lunar cataclysm).

Maksel, Rebecca. "How to discover asteroids in your spare time." *Air & Space Magazine* (March 2011), https://www.airspacemag .com/as-interview/aamps-interview-roy-tucker-112571/?page=3 (this provides the source material for the italicized quote of Roy A. Tucker, which is slightly modified).

Seven Last Words of the Unnamed (2015). Copyright 2015 by Joel Thompson. I am grateful to Mr. Thompson for his work and for his permission to reference his music.

Laura's drawing of an "orbit" is based on the satellite orbit described in Robert E. Gold's *SHIELD: A Comprehensive Earth-Protection System*, https://www.niac.usra.edu/files/library/meetings /annual/mar99/75Gold.pdf. Gold is a physicist at the Johns Hopkins University Applied Physics Laboratory.

It should be noted that *A History of Hazardous Objects* only begins to tell the story of scientists who dedicated their careers to Potentially Hazardous Objects. Beyond Leonid Kulik, Luis Alvarez, Gerald Wasserburg, and Roy A. Tucker, Eugene and Carolyn Shoemaker also figure in this history, as they were the first to detect the Comet Shoemaker-Levy 9. *See,* Murray, Yxta Maya. "I liked looking at the sky." *Chicago Quarterly Review* 34 (2021). Eleanor "Glo" Helin was another titan in this field. *See,* Siegel, Lee. "Planetary scientist mines night sky for asteroids." *New Orleans Times Picayun,* (January 31, 1993).

List of Illustrations

With Gratitude

The author thanks and remembers Fred MacMurray, Thelma Diaz Quinn, Maggie MacMurray, Maria Adastik, Walter Adastik, University of Nevada Press, JoAnne Banducci, Curtis Vickers, the Yaddo Corporation, Diane Mehta, Barbara Friedman, Samira Abbassy, Wang Lu, Anthony Cheung, Sarah Mantell, Coral Saucedo Lomeli, Elaina H. Richardson, Christy Williams, Willapa Bay AIR, Cyndy Hayward, Jeff McMahon, Carrie Gundersdorf, Ernie Wang, Sara Deniz Akant, Kelly Hoppenjans, Mesa Refuge, Peter Barnes, Susan Tillett, Kamala Tully, Joel Thompson, Loyola Law School, Lauren Willis,Yan Slavinskiy, Lighthouse Works, Nate Malinowski, Claudia DeSimone, Jocelyn Saidenberg, Tryn Collins, the Djerassi Foundation, Bradford Morrow, Dr. Eila Skinner, Dr. Joshua Sapkin, the staff of USC Norris Comprehensive Cancer Center, the staff at Keck Hospital of USC, the staff of Providence Saint Joseph Medical Center, Dr. Tina Beth Koopersmith, Kathleen Chapman, Trudi Gershinov, Sara Vélez Mallea, Elizabeth McKenzie, Héctor Tobar, Reneé Vogel, Sarah Preisler, Babs Brown, Kiki Brown, and my dearest, Andrew Brown. I must also give Doug Carlson special thanks for his Herculean editing. In addition, I am grateful to Anne Austin Pearce for her radiant interpretation of Isabella's roses and to Stephen Parise for his exquisite pencil drawing of Ann Hodges.

About the Author

YXTA MAYA MURRAY is a Latinx novelist, art critic, playwright, and law professor. She is the author of eleven books, and the most recent are her novel *God Went Like That* and *We Make Each Other Beautiful: Art, Activism, and the Law.* Murray has won a Whiting Award, an Art Writers Grant, and has been named a fellow at the Huntington Library for her work on radionuclide contamination in Simi Valley, California. Her 2021 novel, *Art is Everything,* was named by *Vox* as one of *The Books That Made Us Think and Act Differently This Year,* and her 2020 book of short stories, *The World Doesn't Work That Way, but It Could* (also published by University of Nevada Press) was named a best book of that year by *BuzzFeed.* She has also published in *The Best American Short Stories* 2021, as well as in numerous literary journals and other publications. She is a 2024–2025 fellow at the Radcliffe Institute for Advanced Study.